The Dream-Escape

By: T.H. Cini

Index

Part 1: Dreams of Linen

Chapter 1: The Discovery

Sunday, June 12, 1983 1:00pm

It was "Garage Sale Day" in Port Perry. It was a beautiful sunny afternoon, and I typically disliked garage sales, as I felt that most of what these folks were selling were silly little trinkets that they couldn't give away to their families; however, I was looking for a set of used golf clubs, and lo and behold, there they were, a set of Vintage Ben Hogan golf clubs sitting out on the front lawn.

"How much for these," I asked the middle-aged woman who sat behind a rickety card table. Beside her was a much older woman. The younger one turned to her and asked: "What did we say we were going to sell Dad's clubs for? Fifty dollars?"

"Oh, give it to him for twenty-five," the old lady said and waved her hand at them as if the clubs were a nuisance to her.

"Twenty-five dollars," the woman confirmed.

"I'll give you fifty. They're worth it!"

"Oh, don't be silly. We said twenty-five. We mean it!" the old lady chirped.

"I'll give you fifty-dollars. Throw in something else if you like, but I'm firm on the fifty dollars.

"Good heavens, you're a stubborn young man," the elderly woman said as she got up from her seat and rounded the table. She wandered around the front lawn, looking at all the remaining items that were scattered on blankets. She held her finger to her chin as she seemed to think desperately what I should be taking to balance out the fifty dollars I insisted on giving.

"Here!" the old woman said, kicking at a leather-bound trunk. "Take this. It's great for storage. Besides, Loraine and I don't have the energy to bring it back inside."

I opened the lid to look at its spaciousness inside. "How old is this?"

"This was my husband's. He had it since before we were married. I would say it's at least fifty years old."

"I see."

I placed the fifty dollars on the table, which the younger woman placed in her tin box. "Thank you for the items. I'll have these out of your way in a jiffy."

*   *   *

Later that afternoon, I brought the clubs into the garage to clean them. I carried the trunk up to my bedroom and placed it in front of my bed like I've seen in many magazines and opened the lid of the trunk to let it air out. I would get these subtle whiffs of a fragrance that I couldn't quite identify. I could really notice it when I re-entered my room after being away from it for a moment or two.

Saturday, July 9, 1983 9:30am

One morning, while organizing my house, I decided to place a few hand-knitted blankets that my mother had made into the trunk. When I opened the lid, I was once again struck by the pleasant-but-distinct scent. I placed the blankets on my bed and leaned over the trunk, searching for where this odor had been coming from. It wasn't offensive by any means.

I leaned back to study the front. The two bottom drawers outside of the trunk were real and not ornamental. I slid my fingernails along the edges of one of the drawers but couldn't manage to pull it open. The locks were real.

I ventured down to the basement to retrieve a flat screwdriver and some other tools that might "jimmy" the locks open. Once back in my bedroom, I knelt in front of the trunk, where I poked and twisted and any other conceivable method to open these locks but to no avail. To continue any further would cause me to damage the locks, so I abandoned the mission, placed the blankets in the trunk and left them there for four months.

Sunday November 20, 1983 8:50pm

It was a very cold November day. The wind howled. When I looked out the window of my old, drafty wood-framed house, I could see the snow come down sideways from the west. The wind was more concerning to me, as I could hear it whistle through the windows. Minutes later, the power went out, turning the house pitch black. I waited for a few seconds so that my eyes could adjust. Once they did, I inched my way towards the kitchen cupboard with my hand stretched out in front of me so that I wouldn't bang my head on anything. Once I found the cupboard, I retrieved a few candles, which I lit with the matches stashed beside them. I lit three of them: one for the kitchen, one for the bathroom and one for me to carry around. My first duty was to get some internal warmth, as the house was quickly becoming cold. I poured a shot of whiskey to sip as I sat in the back room with full view of the walnut trees blowing.

I sipped the whiskey until it was finished and decided to have another one, as it appeared the power wasn't going to be restored anytime soon. Two hours went by, and I was shivering. I thought about driving to my brother Tom's to see if he had power, but it was almost eleven and I didn't want to disturb him. I remembered Moms' blankets that were stored in the trunk, so I took the candle and navigated my way through the dark stairway to my room. I placed the candle on a side table so that I could open the lid of the trunk freely. I placed the first blanket on my bed, knowing that I would need that later tonight if this power stayed off. When I pulled the second blanket out, I heard the sound of something metal bounce on the floor near my feet. I threw the second blanket on the bed, grabbed the candle and knelt down, sliding my palm along the surface of the floorboards. I did this for a few minutes unsuccessfully.

I crouched down with the candle at my eyesight and searched under my bed until I saw a key two feet under my bed. I picked it up and studied it with the light from the candle. It was old. I was uncertain if it was from the trunk or stuck to the blanket from before. *There is only one way to find out!*

I placed the candle back on the side table and stuck the key inside the right drawer. It clicked! *Aha!*

I pulled the drawer open. There were two small wooden boxes in it. I took one and held it up to the candlelight. It was simple, with two hinges and a small latch holding the lid closed. The pleasant odor I was taking in a few months ago was stronger now. *Perhaps this is where that scent was coming from!*

I pulled the latch open. Inside was a piece of frayed yellow linen, nothing else. I picked it up but quickly placed it back, as it appeared that it was going to disintegrate in my fingers if I held it any longer. The odor from the box changed. Its earlier sweet scent had transformed, as I suddenly became sleepy. Still holding the box, I stood up, but almost dropped it and fell back down to my knees. *Oh man! The whiskey must have hit me*. I lifted my foot and steadied it as I pushed myself up so that I could sit on the bed. The whiskey was having an unusual effect as I just wanted to collapse onto my bed. I gingerly placed the still open box on the night table. I lay on my bed and pulled Mom's knitted blanket over me.

With my hands holding the blanket tightly up to my neck, the chill I had earlier had gone away. Maybe I was too tired to think of how cold I was, or maybe it was this blanket doing its job. The wind whistling through the windows changed to a lovely rushing sound. I felt cozy and warm, but something was different. Yes, something was very different. There was that distinct odor again.

Dream # 1

John lay still in bed, sinking deeper in his dream. He was a young boy comfortably tucked under the sheets on a summer's day with the warm breeze blowing through the windows. It wasn't him, though. He knew it wasn't him. He was taking the place of a boy.

"Arthur!"

"Yes, Mommy."

"I just made that bed."

"But I love the smell," he said as he slid from underneath the sheets and plopped onto the floor.

"What smell is that?" mother asked as she tighten the sheets on the bed.

"The fresh clean smell of linen."

"Oh, I should have known. Now go out and get some fresh air while it's still nice out. Not too far, though. We are supposed to get a storm tonight."

Arthur turned to look at the thin drapes blowing high in the air from the force of the summer wind, rushing through the windows.

He ran down the stairs, placed his sandals on and ran to the creek, which was about two hundred yards away from his house. He stopped at about halfway to look back at his tiny clothes blowing in the summer breeze before continuing. The creek was the perfect spot, as it had an apple tree just a few yards away. When he sat under the tree in the summer, he could hear the splashing water against the rocks. He took his sandals off, rolled up his pants and walked into the creek, feeling the fresh cool water run past his tiny legs. He bent over, stepping carefully on the cold stones, looking for crayfish to catch. With his hands cupped and ready, he scanned the bottom of the creek. Arthur did this for a few yards downstream, then turned to face upstream, when something white and bright caught the corner of his eye. He slowly stood up to see a young woman standing on the edge of the other side of the creek, facing him.

"Hello," he said, standing still as he was startled from her sudden appearance.

The young lady stood there staring down at him from the ledge of the embankment. She wore what looked like a white nightgown, which he found odd for mid-day. She had brown hair and slate-gray eyes that Arthur found strange but not frightening.

"Do you live around here?" Arthur asked.

"Your name is Arthur Driscoll, isn't it?"

"Yes. How did you know my name?"

"I know many things about you. I've seen you but not as you are now. I've seen you as a grown man."

"What do you mean?"

"You silly boy." The young woman smiled. "You don't recognize this?" She said, pulling the edges of her nighty with both hands, creating the image of a puffy dress. She let the edges drop.

"I don't know who you are, ma'am," he answered and then walked to the other side of the embankment. He grabbed his sandals, walked back towards his house, turning around twice to see her still standing there watching him.

When he entered the house, he was about to tell his mother what, or rather, who he saw, but he didn't. He raced up stairs and ran to his mother's bedroom window, which had a perfect view of the creek. Once he got to the window, he pushed her drapes aside to see the twisted apple tree and nothing else. She had disappeared!

John wakes

Monday, November 21, 1983 4:07am

I sat up, quickly realizing that all the lights in the room were on. I was sweating from the heat of the room and the knitted blanket that was covering me. I quickly threw off the blanket and slid out of my bed to blow out the candle. I felt a little woozy, so I sat back on the bed. I rubbed my forehead, as I had a slight headache.

That was a weird dream. I've never had a dream like that before. I was living the dream of a young boy named Arthur, but I knew it wasn't me. It was someone else a long time ago. And that young woman with the slate eyes. That was unusual.

I reached for the clock. It read seven minutes after four in the morning, so I shut off all the lights in the house, changed into my pajamas. I took the little box, closed it and put it back in the trunk where I found it and went back to sleep.

Chapter 2: No Whiskey

Saturday November 26, 1983 11:31 pm

A few days had gone by since the night the power went out. The dream I had was firmly implanted in my mind. I remember the details of that dream vividly, though I would only remember fragments of other dreams. I made the decision early in the evening to bring out that box with the linen.

I dressed for bed, turned the tiny lamp on my night table, grabbed the box and placed it beside the lamp. I could already take in the sweet scent before I opened it. I made a point of not having any beer or wine and definitely no whiskey that night. I sat on the edge of my bed and opened the box. I took in one long inhale of its scent and slid myself under the covers of my cozy bed. I could feel my body become heavy as that familiar intoxicating feeling came over me.

Dream # 2

"Merry Christmas!" the woman behind the counter said as she passed the neatly wrapped box across the counter.

John stood there for a moment, collected his thoughts and headed towards the door. He looked up at the bell as it rang when he opened the front door. It was already dark out, and the snow was dropping like white down-feathers, slowly hovering from above. He grabbed the lapel of his coat and pulled it over his neck and chest as the snow left tiny wet droplets on his nose and face. As he maneuvered his way through the busy sidewalks, each streetlamp started to illuminate one by one. They flickered for a few seconds until they fully illuminated. He continued until he reached a side street, which was strangely familiar. He opened a large, heavy metal door that shut loudly behind him. He continued to the end of the dank, yellow hallway, which brought him to a stairwell, which he climbed up rapidly, floor by floor until he reached the top.

He recognized the door, which he quickly approached. The number on the wood was seven-hundred-and eighteen. John found it remarkable how natural this all came to him. He rapped quietly and waited patiently until he heard the sound of footsteps approaching. The door opened slowly, stopping when the chain latch caught. Beyond was a young face with gray eyes and plump red lips. It closed slightly and then opened all the way, exposing a young woman who John recognized. But he wasn't John.

"Come in Arthur." The young woman turned her back as she walked away.

The woman's name came to him.

"Hello, Ana."

Ana had the fireplace going, which was very cozy, but he left his coat and gloves on holding the parcel under his arm. He started to feel anxious and unwanted. Ana studied him with her slate eyes.

"Is that for me?" she asked.

"Yes," Arthur answered and passed her the box.

Ana finally lightened up, smiling as she unwrapped the parcel. She took out the garment and hung it high in the air as she quickly stood up to show it off. It was a white, linen nightgown, with an embroidered collar.

"I love it!" she said, running towards Arthur and giving him a cold kiss on the cheek. She stepped onto her red chair and held it up high. "It's a little long, but I love it. Let me try it on."

Ana rushed out of the main room to change into her new nightgown.

"You're going to take your coat and gloves off, aren't you," Ana hollered from her bedroom.

"Yes," Arthur responded with hesitation.

He slowly took off his jacket and gloves, knowing that he couldn't stay long. He glanced up at the mantel clock which was just about to strike four in the morning. He had one more hour, maybe two.

"There! What do you think?" Ana expressed while twirling in front of him.

The nightgown fit her perfectly. It pleased Arthur that he had made such a good choice and was able to make her happy. The light of the fireplace shone through the dress, exposing her lovely figure, which further pleased him. Ana held the edges of the nightgown up as if about to curtsy, which gave him an immediate flash-back.

"What is it, Arthur?"

Arthur stared out into oblivion for a moment before he came back.

"It's nothing."

The clock chimed four in the morning, causing Arthur to glance at the clock. He immediately regretted doing this as it upset Ana every time he checked.

"Oh . . ." Ana expressed as she stomped out of the room. Time, time, time . . . you're always checking the time."

Arthur placed his hands together and looked down at the floor with guilt. He tried to think of a comforting response, but it never came to him. Ana rushed back into the front room with a pair of scissors.

"There's an extra piece of material on the back that's bothering me. Can you see it?" she asked turning her back to him.

Arthur stood up and checked the back where he could see an extra piece of fabric that didn't have any purpose. It was sewed to the back but was hanging loose.

"Yes, I see it. It's the back. Take it off, and you'll see it."

Ana left to go back into her room.

"I found it." She was silent for a moment while she did her cutting. She called from her room: "Arthur?"

"Yes, sweetheart."

"How long will you stay tonight?"

"Another hour," he replied, gritting his teeth in anticipation of her response.

Ana was quiet.

After a few moments, she whisked her way into the main room like a ballerina, pointing her toe in the air and then dropped it.

To Arthur's surprise, she was smiling. She leaned in for a kiss and then placed a two-inch, by two-inch piece of linen into his hands.

"Take this," she said with a grin.

"What do you mean?"

"Take it with you."

"How?" he asked.

"Just like you do with the money. Fold in neatly and place it in the palm of your hand before you go to sleep. That way, you will make it back here every night."

"OK. I will," he said with a slight hesitation.

"What are you worried about? Your wife finding out about us?" she said studying Arthur.

"She's not going to find out about our dreams together."

Ana plopped herself in her chair and raised her foot up to Arthur's chair, placing it between his knees.

"This way, we can dream together every night, as opposed to, when you just-so-happened to come into my dream."

Arthur sat in his chair, holding the piece of cloth in his hand, thinking about the opportunity of seeing Ana every night. He also knew that the dream-escape he was about to encounter nightly would take away from his conscious life, thus his hesitation. He was mixed with emotions, but as Ana was still holding her gaze, waiting for a response, he knew he had to provide a positive one.

"That's a great idea. Let's see if this works."

"It will work. Don't worry."

The couple spent another hour together, sitting by the warm fire. Later on, while there was silence, Arthur peered down to see Ana's toes wriggle while she had it placed on his chair. He wanted to take her foot in his hand and rub it, but his arm and hands were too heavy to move, which frustrated him as he just wanted to touch her skin. Each evening he had dreams of Ana, he would desire to touch her, but just as he was about to make his move, he couldn't.

"Arthur," Ana whispered, but he was slipping away. "Arthur. You're drifting on me."

Ana got up from her chair, opened the palm of his hand to confirm the piece of linen was still there, then closed his hand tightly.

"See you tomorrow night Arthur," Ana expressed while holding his fisted hand tightly.

John wakes

Sunday November 27, 1983 5:24am

I woke with a rush. I sat up quickly and checked my hand: clenched closed. I slowly opened it -- but no piece of linen. Disappointed, I leaned towards the night table to see the small piece of fabric tucked in the box I had placed there the night before.

I rubbed my eyes and eventually got up and made a coffee. Once awake, I search my kitchen drawer for a pad and paper and wrote out, in as much detail as I could remember, each of my last two dreams. Even though both remained vivid in my mind, I didn't want to lose any of it.

Chapter 3: The Dream-Escape

Sunday November 27, 1983 11:04pm

I retrieved the wooden box from the trunk and placed it on the night table until I was settled in bed. I studied the open box for a moment before the odor seeped into my nostrils, my lungs and eventually into my bloodstream, creating its familiar effect.

Dream # 3

Ana opened the door part-way making sure it was Arthur.

"It worked!" Ana was so delighted; she danced around her room in her white linen nightgown.

"Take off your coat. I want to see you without your coat."

Arthur carefully removed his coat and hung it on the dining room chair. He was nervous and excited, as he was experiencing an Ana he hadn't seen before. He stood still watching as she slid herself closer to him, placing her hands on his chest, moving them up and down. He jumped, as her hands were icy.

"Are they cold, my dear?"

"A little, but it's OK."

"Put your arms around me. I want to feel your warmth."

Arthur placed his arms around her and pulled her tightly against his body. She was extremely cold, so it took a few moments for him to enjoy her embrace. As he held her, she brought her face against his neck, giving him cold wet kisses along his neck above his shirt collar. He eventually looked into her eyes, which brought their lips tighter for that long-anticipated first kiss. Arthur felt the transformation of his feeling towards her. The kiss was more exhilarating than her stare. But that wasn't all transforming him; he felt the heat from his body transfer to hers. He was falling for her, so he wanted to give away his heat. He could tell she was craving it.

Once she had warmed up, he could finally appreciate her body, rubbing his hands up and down her back as they kissed deeper.

"Let's lie on the floor in front of the fireplace." Ana took his hand and knelt on the decorated carpet in front of the fire. She grabbed a pillow from the chair and placed it on the carpet, guiding Arthur's head onto it. Arthur quickly glanced up at the clock, which read four-twenty in the morning.

They lay on the floor for an hour, facing each other, Arthur running his hand from her hip up to her ribcage, her body becoming warmer as they embraced.

"I'm sorry I was so mean to you last night. I really *do* like this place," Ana said as she touched the side of his face. "Do you think she knows?"

"No. There is no way for her to know. It's *my* dream."

Ana's expression changed.

"I know. But what about the money? Will she notice?"

"She won't. I'm the one who manages our finances. She has no way of knowing that either."

"OK," Ana responded and gave Arthur a kiss.

Arthur and Ana lay there, embracing, but something different was happening to Arthur that night. Not only was he drifting off into his conscious state, he was losing body heat. Arthur brought her body tighter, wanting to kiss her deeper, but she broke the kiss, her body stiffening as she pulled away slightly.

"What is it?"

"He came again."

"Who?"

"You know. The man with the monocle. He said the rent was due."

"Oh, for heaven's sake." Arthur sat up.

Ana was sensitive to Arthur's change in mood. She bit her bottom lip as she apparently thought about her next comment. "Will you bring some money tomorrow? He made it seem that it was urgent."

Arthur leaned against his chair. He started rubbing his arm to get warm.

"I feel cold, and I'm going to slip away soon sweetheart," he said, getting up to put his coat on, then sat in his usual chair and closed his eyes.

"Arthur," Ana called.

He was quickly drifting off, so he didn't answer right away.

"Arthur!" she called again.

"Huh," he murmured.

"You will bring the two-hundred dollars tomorrow night, won't you my dear?"

"Yes, sweetheart." Arthur answered with eyes still closed.

John wakes

Monday November 28, 1983 5:42am

It was still dark. My eyes rolled around as I lay perfectly still, shivering under my layers of blankets. I could hear the thunder of the snow plow run along my street. I checked the window to see that there were several inches of snow that came that night. I wasn't tired enough to go back to sleep, but I was still very cold, so I grabbed my house coat, made a cup of coffee and made notes about my recent dream of Arthur and Ana.

After I made my notes, I fell back against my chair and thought about the dream. It was obvious to me that this "Arthur" was having an affair, of-sorts, with Ana. He must have been married during his conscious state. *Who is this Arthur? Was he the late husband of that old woman I bought the trunk from? The more and more I dream of him, the more I need to get to know him. It seemed absurd that he would fall in love with a woman in a dream. It almost sounds like he was escaping his conscious state to be with Ana. Maybe Arthur never existed. Is Arthur just a dream, within my dream? What is it about that piece of linen?*

Chapter 4: The Man with the Monocle

Saturday, December 3rd, 1983 9:37pm

The days went by, and I didn't take out the box, but the memories of the dream didn't fade. I became increasingly curious who Arthur was and what was going to happen next, so I planned another dream that night. It was only nine-thirty, but I was tired from shoveling snow. I brought out the box, popped open the lid, took a large inhale and off I went.

Dream # 4

Once Arthur reached the large metal door, he removed his tightly held fist from his coat to look once more at the bundle of cash held in his hand. He shoved the bundle into his side coat pocket and pulled the door. Arthur didn't climb the staircase this time. Instead, he walked briskly down the hall, past the main foyer until he reached the end of the hallway. The light in that end of the hallway was burnt out, which made Arthur a little nervous, as it had been a while since he had seen the landlord.

He stopped in front of door number one-hundred-and-one. He smelled cigarette smoke creeping from the cracks between the door and the frame. He knocked. As he waited, he heard a parrot's squawk from inside the apartment. Arthur had temporarily forgotten about the annoying bird. Eventually the door unlatched, displaying the man with the monocle on his right eye. The man had greasy, slicked back hair, a thin moustache and a French accent.

"I see you got my message," he said, flashing his sly grin. "Come in. Come in." He opened the door and signaled Arthur to sit at the tiny kitchen table. There was a cigarette smoldering on the ashtray, which the man picked up, squinted, before taking a drag. He exhaled before finally addressing Arthur.

"It appears your circumstances have changed," he said, smoothing the palm of his hand along his shiny hair slicked back with pomade. "Your mistress has stayed here much longer than you had originally told me. That is why I had to pay a visit." He took another puff of his cigarette, not making eye contact with Arthur, this time, leaving it dangling from his mouth.

Arthur was about to reach into his side pocket to remove the cash when the parrot let out a whistle.

"Here." Arthur pulled out his money, opening it exposing the cash that was neatly stack in his hand.

The man took it and began to count it.

"I hope you don't mind," he said, while holding the cash in his hand.

"Go ahead. It's all there."

The man held the bundle in the palm of one hand, while pulling each bill out of the other, counting it as he lay each on the table. While he did this, the parrot made clicking sounds from the other room, which Arthur found unnerving.

The man eventually stopped counting.

"This is fine," he said banging the money on the tabletop to square it up. "So . . ." he stuck the tip of his tongue out and picked a piece of tobacco off it. "How long do you intend on keeping this place for her?" He looked up at Arthur.

"Does it matter?" Arthur stood up now that their business was finished.

"No." The man with the monocle remained seated. He held his cigarette with one hand and slid the palm of his other hand along his greasy hair again. "Just know, that this will only last a few more nights."

"What's a few more nights?" Arthur was growing impatient with the man.

"Oh . . . let's see." He kept stroking his hair, front to back a few times before answering. "Five nights."

"All right," Arthur replied turning to leave. "Please don't bother Ana. I'll come see you before the fifth night."

"Is that her name?" the man with the monocle replied, grinning his crooked yellow teeth.

"I will come see you before the fifth night," Arthur replied.

"Mr. Driscoll?"

Arthur turned, as he was now extremely irritated.

"You're looking awfully tired. Are you sure you can last another five more nights?"

Arthur didn't answer. He opened the door and closed it behind him.

After closing the door, Arthur heard the parrot squawk what sounded like "dead man," which caused him to halt briefly before heading up the six flights of stairs to see Ana. Once in front of her door, Arthur felt a chill and rubbed his arms them before he knocked.

Ana opened the door and peeked through the opening like she did every night. She wore her lovely linen nightgown and showed it off to Arthur like it was the first time she wore it, but Arthur didn't mind. He loved her so much he was willing to play along with her fancies.

"Arthur!" Ana exclaimed. "You're looking tired tonight." Ana started to remove his coat, but he was still feeling a chill.

"I think I'll leave it on, sweetheart. I've got shivers."

Ana was persistent however and continued to open his jacket, pressing her icy body against his, which drained him of even more heat.

"Can you light a fire, sweetheart? I'm going to use your bathroom."

He strode toward the tiny bathroom at the end of the hallway. He twisted the light switch on, producing a yellow glow from the tungsten light, which was set directly above the dirty mirror. The mirror was showing signs of de-silvering throughout, which made it difficult to see. He leaned closer to study his pale face, tracing the large gray circles under his eyes. He surprised himself as to how awful he looked. Arthur was not himself. He was cold, tired and wanted to be anywhere but there. He sat on the edge of the tub, thinking about what he was doing to himself, hoping the night would end quickly and thought: *If I could only be back in bed with his wife.*

Arthur sighed, pushed himself off the tub and carried on down the hallway to the front room, hoping to get some heat from the fireplace before drifting off.

"Sweetheart!" Arthur blurted out, upon discovering the fireplace had not been lit.

Ana looked up at him from her red chair with a look of despair.

"I don't have any wood left, my dear."

"Oh no," Arthur said, plopping himself in the chair, feeling defeated.

He sat in his chair, shivering, wanting to leave, but his body wasn't ready for him to drift off yet. Instead, he sat there, shivering and shivering, and shivering . . . . . .

John wakes

Sunday, December 4th, 1983 4:13am

I woke on my side, in a fetal position, shivering as Arthur did in his dream of him. I threw off the covers and ran down the stairs to check if the furnace was broken, but it was running just fine. The thermostat was set to where I had left it, so quickly made my way upstairs, crawled into bed and tried to warm up as quickly as I could. *That was the most unsettling of all the dreams I've had!*

I didn't end up falling back asleep, and it took hours for my body temperature to feel normal again.

Chapter 5: Arthur's world

Friday, December 9, 1983 10:31pm

I needed to sleep all week without the linen box open. Although I found these dreams exciting, it was exhausting me. I could only enter Arthur's dream-world on the weekends now. Even then, I was taking naps in the afternoon, as I don't think I was actually sleeping when I entered his dreams.

I opened the box containing the linen, took in its sweet scent and dozed off.

John wakes

Saturday, December 10, 1983 2:10am

I woke in a panic. The room was pitch black. I turned my lamp on and checked my clock. It was ten-after-two in the morning. *What? No dream? What happened?*

I felt disappointed. I even panicked, thinking that might be the end of the dreams. I sat up in my bed for a minute, wondering what to do, when I recalled the second linen dream when Arthur clenched the fabric in the palm of his hand before falling asleep. I studied the open box before reaching in. I delicately took the frail piece and clenched it tightly. I shut off the light and shifted myself down in my bed, yanking the covers up to my chin, being careful not to release the linen from my hand. I lay still, taking in the sweet fragrance that swirled around my room until it entered my nostrils, providing me the intoxication I needed to fade into slumber.

John's Dream-Escape

John stood on the sidewalk motionless until he found his bearings. He watched as the streetlights flickered on like he had seen many nights before. His recollection of his surroundings began to pour in, causing him to turn and walk farther up the street. He recognized the dark side street and continued until he was in front of the large metal door. He tugged it and entered the stairwell.

He quietly made his way up the staircase to the seventh floor. Once in front of that familiar door, he took a deep breath and knocked quietly. There was silence for a moment, causing him to lift his clenched hand again, but he stopped upon hearing footsteps approach. He took a step back and listened to a doorknob click when turned. It opened, exposing a middled-aged man with wiry red hair.

"Yes." The man stared at him through the opening.

John recognized the man in the mirror as Arthur; the man he was following in his dreams. John stuttered in his response.

"I . . . I'm here to see Ana."

"Ana?" The man's faced changed. His eyebrows pinched together causing one to rise higher than the other. His blue eyes looked angry as if the name "Ana" had upset him. John was anxious. He rubbed his hands to maintain warmth.

Arthur peered down at John's hands and back up.

"How do you know Ana?"

John was not prepared to answer such a question and panicked.

"I . . . I've made a mistake. I'm so sorry to have bothered you. I'll be on my way," John replied and quickly turned to face the stairwell.

"Stop!" Arthur demanded and un-latched the door, bringing himself into the hallway.

John stood still, watching as Arthur looked behind him quickly.

"Come here."

John reluctantly paced his way back towards him. Arthur wasn't as confrontational, and his body language wasn't intimidating anymore.

"You're alive, aren't you!"

"I don't know what you mean."

Arthur looked behind him again and waved.

"You better come in."

John entered the room, but it was still cold. Arthur was a stalky man with wiry red hair. He was wearing a white t-shirt with suspenders and dress pants. He motioned for John to sit in the familiar red chair.

"Please, take a seat." Arthur had a very gravelly voice.

Arthur took a seat where Ana would have normally sat and watched his guest look around at the empty fireplace and the clock on the mantel, which read a little after four in the morning.

"Are you cold?"

"A little."

"Just as I thought. You're alive," he said, glancing at the clock quickly before facing me again. "You will need to doze off soon."

John straightened himself up, before speaking.

"You're Arthur, aren't you?"

The man stared at John for a moment before cracking a smile.

"How would you know a thing like that." He pinched his eyebrows together again and then pointed his finger at me. "You *know* something." The man stood up, rounded his chair. "You're not telling me everything, boy. Yes. That's my name. You better spill your guts; otherwise, you're going get yourself into a heap of trouble." He leaned on the back the chair. "So, start talking."

He knew he had done something very wrong by entering this world. It was one thing to be in another man's dream, but now he was in his own dream-escape, and not a pleasant one. John remembered the linen that was still firmly stuck in his fist, so he turned it over and released his grip, exposing the cloth.

"I'd better start with this."

"Where did you get that?"

Arthur approached him, leaning over to pluck the tiny piece from his hand to study it. He walked in front of the fireplace, carefully positioned it on the mantel, trying to flatten it with his fingers.

"I came across it by accident," John said as Arthur's back was towards him. "I bought a trunk from an old lady and her daughter, and there it was. In a small box."

Arthur remained quiet as John continued his story.

"I opened the box and fell asleep; that's when . . ."

John paused, as he wasn't sure how Arthur was going to react.

"Yes." Arthur turned around. "And?"

"That's when I entered . . . a dream."

Arthur walked behind his chair and leaned on it, like he had before.

"Keep going."

John told Arthur about each of the four dreams, the detail of Ana, the man with the monocle and of course Arthur. Arthur's hostility subsided as John explained the intrigue of the dreams. He stood silent as John told of how he discovered the box in the trunk. He felt a little ashamed about entering Arthur's private dreams.

"I apologize for having intruded. I really didn't know if any of it was real."

Arthur took his seat and finally made eye contact with him. John sunk in his chair looking as though he was about to be reprimanded. Arthur crossed his arms and stared at John with a furrowed forehead.

"How did you even get in here? I mean, this building," Arthur asked.

"Through the side door, as you did."

"What's your name, boy?"

"John."

John was feeling sick with worry. He knew he broke many rules tonight. He started feeling cold and tired, shifting his eyes towards the mantel. It was quarter-to-five.

43

"All right. You've got maybe another hour before you drift off, so listen carefully."

John nodded.

"Ana was a thief. She was planted here by the man with the eyeglass."

"How was Ana a thief?"

"They were a team. He got my money. She got my body heat. Oh yeah, she was easy to fall for. I was a sucker for it." Arthur paced the room. "I had many dreams when I was a child, but one of them stuck with me, the one you envisioned with me as a young boy. That one stuck with me for years, and then one night, while I was married, I saw her again, in a dream. I met her while I was wondering on that street. It was constantly snowing, and the streetlights were just turning on. We would walk up and down the street together every night until one evening, she asked me to see the man with the eyeglass. He owned the building and would put her up if I paid, which I did. I placed the money in my fist, while sleeping beside my wife, and was able to cross over with it."

John watched as Arthur continued to explain.

"So, here I am, stuck in this . . . sort of purgatory. I know I was unfaithful to my wife. I'm guilty of it."

Arthur continued pacing and not making eye contact. "Ana killed me. Yes, I'm a dead man." He finally stopped pacing and looked down at John. "You see, I didn't touch her right away. When I eventually did, she sucked the heat from my body, bit, by bit, until one day . . . . I didn't wake up. I didn't wake up in my bed, beside my wife. I woke up here." Arthur pointed to my chair. "Right there, in that chair you're in. Ana was gone. I guess she got what she wanted."

"I'm sorry," John responded.

"Don't be sorry for me," Arthur snapped. "It's my own doing."

"I don't understand. Why did she steal your heat?"

"So, she. . ." Arthur stared at me, but didn't finish.

"What?"

Arthur's face changed as he stood in front of John, watching John's warm breath, puff into the air.

"Stand up, boy."

John did.

Arthur stepped closer to John, which made him feel awkward.

"You've been most honest. I want to thank you."
Arthur reached out his hand. "I'd like to shake
your hand."

John took Arthur's cold hand in his. After a
moment, Arthur's grip became tighter continuing
to hold John's hand, which caused John to pull it
back, but Arthur didn't give-way.

"What are you doing?" John asked, but Arthur
tightened his grip even more.

"Let go, please."

John pulled back harder, but Arthur didn't let go,
instead he placed his other hand over John's to
further prevent him from releasing it. The two
men wrestled each other until they fell to the
floor. John was becoming increasingly cold as he
lay with his back on the floor, with Arthur holding
him down. Arthur's eyes lit up as if becoming
rejuvenated, gritting his teeth with delight.

"My God. I'm alive. I can feel it through you,"
Arthur said, placing his cold hand over John's
neck.

John lay there, becoming weaker and colder. His
body shook until he eventually lost the strength
to fight. His eyes closed with exhaustion.

Chapter 6: Stuck!

John sat up quickly realizing he was still in his dream and in the same room, but no Arthur. Panic set in as he scanned the floor around him. He got to his feet and checked the fireplace mantel. No linen. The mantel clock read eight-thirty.

"Oh no. It's morning. I'm still stuck in this dream."

John plopped himself on the chair and replayed the night's events through his head, when suddenly a thought came to him. He rushed to the bathroom and stood in front of the dirty mirror and let out a huge breath. No fog. He quickly brought his hand to his mouth in shock.

"I'm dead."

He made his way back to the main room, staggering along the way, realizing Arthur had stolen his heat, leaving him dead and stuck in his own dream. He was in major trouble as he realized there was no out, no piece of linen to bring him back. John brought his hands to his head, pressing the palms of his hands onto his forehead.

"Think John, think!"

* * *

John sat in that apartment, thinking of what to do. As the days passed by, he discovered many things in his dead-dream-like state. He discovered that the daytime was horrifically bright, which his eyes couldn't handle. That would explain why the blinds were always shut tight. During his time there, he was never disturbed by anyone, which he took comfort in, especially as he expected a visit from the man with the monocle, but strangely enough, he never paid a visit. In evening time, especially after ten in the evening, things were energetic for him. He would rest during the day and come alive at night. He also discovered that he was never hungry or thirsty or even cold for that matter. There was one thing he did, however, begin to crave and that was live people. It wasn't companionship, or sex; it was something else. He couldn't quite put his finger on it, but he knew he must have it.

One evening, he was too restless to look at the four walls of the apartment and decided to venture out of his building. John put on his coat and took the staircase down, being quiet until he reached the large metal door. He opened it, to see nighttime in the snowy street he'd walked along many times. He turned and let the door close, without it locking. He had trouble containing his smile as he could see pedestrians scurry back and forth along the snowy street. Lights flickered inside each lamp housing. He watched as the snowflakes fell one-by-one from the sky and on his face.

He walked up and down the street, passing many citizens of this dead-dream-world of his, but he wasn't interested in them. No, he was searching for something specific, something very specific. He continued to wander, never feeling tired. This continued until it finally happened. John's face lit up as his eyes finally found her.

There she was. A visitor to his dream. She sat on the bench, watching John approach her. He studied her as she looked up at him with her brown eyes. Everything about what she was dreaming all flowed into him. It was incredibly natural for him.

"Hello, Mary."

Mary stood up, but John didn't dare offer his cold hand. He kept it firmly in his coat pockets.

"Hello, John. I've been expecting you," she stated.

"Come, let's go for a walk."

Mary tucked her arm in around the elbow of John's arm, bringing herself closer to him. Mary had long brown hair and brown eyes that almost smiled when she looked up at John.

"I'm happy you came tonight," Mary said as she studied John's face as she walked along. "I've come in for several nights waiting for you, and here you are. Just as I expected."

John could feel her warmth as she held his arm in hers. He knew from the experience with Ana and Arthur that Arthur was hooked once he seen her in the first dream. He felt that Mary was waiting for him, but he had to play along, and he would eventually get what he had been craving for.

"You were expecting me, too?" John asked.

"Yes, I knew it was you as soon as you approach the bench." Mary stopped and faced him, releasing her arm and placing her hands on his chest. "Hold me please. I'm getting cold."

John wrapped his arms around her, bringing her closer. He peered up at the gray sky, watching the snowflakes drop onto their coats and faces, sticking on to their eyelashes. John must play this slowly and carefully. He knew the game and that it would take time to gain her trust and desire for him. Witnessing how Ana manipulated Arthur made this ordeal easier for John, but it was so much his character that was driving this; it was survival.

"Will you return tomorrow?"

"Yes. I will dream of you tomorrow." Mary smiled, pressed her face against John's chest and closed her eyes. He allowed her to rest against him as he thought about the process. He was always on the other side of a dream ending and drifting off, but he never witnessed this himself, so when Mary slid away while in his grasp, he felt the loss and emptiness. Mary's presence had dissipated; the touch, the smell of her hair and of course her warmth had left him. John was sad for that few moments before his mood changed to anticipation for the next evening. He darted for the metal door and spent the rest of the next day thinking about seeing her again.

*   *   *

John checked the mantel clock, which read two-thirty in the morning. He knew it was probably too early, but he didn't want to miss out on seeing Mary, so he made his way to the street and then finally to the bench, but no Mary. He paced up and down the asphalt, glancing at the clock in the main tower, which chimed three. He took a seat on the same bench Mary had arrived at the night before. While he was seated, something occur to him that hadn't the night before. Was Mary was going have a dream about him that night? He now appreciated how Ana's idea of the linen piece would have brought her comfort. Perhaps John could recreate that trick somehow.

As John sat on the bench waiting, he studied the minute hand on the clock. He would stare at it, minute-by-minute, watching it move slowly until he felt it. He felt her warmth.

"Oh, John. You waited for me," Mary said, placing her hands on his arm.

"Of course! I wouldn't miss seeing you for the world."

John was happy to see her. His happiness mixed with his desire for her warmth.

"Aren't you cold?" Mary asked. "You don't even have a scarf."

"I'm fine like this."

Mary took her hand and reached into John's pocket, searching for his bare hand.

"Good God! You're freezing!"

John pulled away quickly. The sudden jolt of heat was exhilarating for him, but he feared of what was to come of it.

"What's wrong?"

"I get cold hands," he said with embarrassment. "Here. Place your hand on my arm, like you did last night."

Mary relented and scooted closer to John and snuggled on the bench watching the passersby. John sat still, letting Mary play out her dream. While he waited patiently, he noticed the tiny shop where Arthur bought the nightgown for Ana. Life in that dream seemed so innocent at first. The memories were haunting.

"I could snuggle with you all night," Mary expressed, closing her eyes briefly before opening them to look up at John. "Don't you have a place we could have more privacy? The street always seems so busy."

"I have a room in that apartment right over there," John gestured. "Would you like to see it?"

"Yes, I want to be with you, privately."

John stood up.

"Take my arm."

*　　*　　*

John closed the door behind him and studied Mary as she roamed the room.

"Cozy little spot."

"Yes."

"Can you start the fire?" she asked as she twirled around to face John.

"I don't have any wood. Sorry."

"That's a shame. I guess, I'll leave my coat on then." Mary stood still in front of the mantle, perhaps waiting for John's manners to kick in.

"Have a seat. Please," John gestured to the chair where he had sat so many times as John and Arthur.

John took his coat off and sat across from Mary.

"You're not cold?"

"No. I'm used to it," he answered, not making eye contact with her, because he had to conceal his reasoning as to why he was never cold.

John let her ramble on about her conscious life. The more she divulged, the more John knew he had her. The more relaxed she was with him, the more she spoke of her boring life as a housewife in a loveless marriage. Mary was escaping from her conscious life, much like Arthur did. As he listened, he was planning his next move. The wheels in his head turned while he contemplated what he wanted most, her heat! As he sat there, silently scheming, something happened that John had not had to deal with before. An unexpected knock at the door.

John looked at Mary with surprise.

"Who could that be?" Mary asked, getting up.

"Please. Sit down."

So many things ran through John's mind as he paced the twenty-odd-feet between his chair and the door. *Could it be Ana? Is she returning?*

He heard another knock before opening the door until the latch caught. It was the man with the monocle.

"Yes?" John answered.

"I see you have company."

John didn't know how to answer, as this was the first time he had seen the man in his own state. *Why hadn't this man come before.*

"Yes. Can I help you?"

"You! Help me?" the man said laughing with his finger pointed at John. "I am the owner of this building, so, yes. You will be doing more than help. You must . . ." he stopped studying the latch holding the door, only so far open. "Do you mind?"

John unlatched the door, letting the man in.

"Pardon me, Mademoiselle," he said nodding towards Mary, then turning to John. "Monsieur?" he asked me.

"Mr. Randall."

"Monsieur Randall. How do I say this in the politest of ways?" the man said, sliding the palm of his hand along his slick black hair. "I don't allow guests here, without . . . payment," the man flashed his yellow crooked teeth at me.

"Sir, I don't have . . ." John started but was quickly cut-off.

The man turned to Mary. "Perhaps . . ."

She searched her coat pockets fruitlessly, stopping with the shaking of her head.

"I'm sorry. I don't have anything with me."

The man with the monocle, swung back to stare at John, still sporting his sly grin. "I'll give you a couple of nights. Come see me in apartment one-0-one with the money. Two-hundred should tide you over for a few nights."

The man reached for the door.

"Mademoiselle, monsieur," he expressed before quietly closing the door behind him.

Not only was John piecing together the events that took place between Arthur and Ana and the man with the monocle, but he was witnessing the deal in action. John was cornered, probably like Ana was. He had to play along, so he needed to have Mary bring the money over from her conscious state to her dream. Yes. The plan was forming. He would have her bring the money, he would pay for rent, buy some wood, then steal her heat, but John needed to focus on Mary, as she looked distressed.

"John. How will you get the money?"

"I don't know. I don't have any here. Maybe . . ."

"What?"

'Maybe you can bring it over." John knelt in front of Mary ready to detail his plan. "Will you try something for me?"

"Of course."

"Place two-one-hundred-dollar bills in your fist tightly, before going to sleep. Maybe it will carry over. Will you try that for me?"

"Yes, my sweet," Mary said as she ran her hand over his face. "Your face is so cold." She studied John's face for a moment, before falling back in her chair and closing her eyes.

He watched her drift off into her conscious state, slowly disappearing, leaving him empty once again.

* * *

John heard the knock on the door and immediately panicked for fear it was the man with the monocle. He opened the door, exposing Mary's smiling face between the eight inches of opening.

"Well, hello. Come on in!"

Mary could barely conceal her smile as she reached out her fist, exposing the two-hundred-dollars.

"It worked!" John exclaimed with such happiness.

"Wait!" Mary reached out her other hand exposing another two hundred. "For the wood, for the fireplace."

"Have a seat. I'm going to see the man right away, so I can enjoy the rest of the evening with you."

John scurried down the hallway and down the staircase to apartment one-hundred-and one. He knew the man was there as he could smell the smoke from outside of the door. John gave the door a knock and waited as he heard the parrot let out a squawk. John waited while the man fiddled with the door before it opened.

"Come in please. I hope you like parrots," the man said, gesturing to John to sit across from him.

John looked around the room, taking in its familiar surroundings.

"Do you mind?" the man said, pulling a cigarette from his pack.

"Not at all."

"For yourself," he asked shoving the cigarette between his lips before lighting it.

"No, thank you."

"So," he exhaled his smoke before finishing. "Looks like you found yourself some warm company." When the man grinned, his crooked yellow teeth resembled that of fenceposts on an old fence, with one post leaning one way, another post leaning the other.

"Yes, that's right," John replied, but was curious how he knew this. This man knew more than he led on, or John was just naïve.

"Well." The man took another puff before placing his cigarette in the ashtray. "That's your business. But I know what you are up to. It's no secret to me."

"Oh?" John said, leaning back in his chair, waiting for the man to continue.

"You want to return. You want your life back." The man picked up his cigarette, took a puff and placed it back in the ashtray. "You lost your normal life to . . . someone." The man tapped his lips as he was thinking. "It wasn't Ana, was it? No, it was Ana's victim, the Irish fellow, with the red hair," he said raising his hand over the top of his head. "I don't know how that happened. How you met those two is a mystery to me. You stumbled into their dreams somehow."

The man leaned back studying my face, waiting for a response.

"What happened to Ana?"

The man with the monocle picked up his cigarette but didn't take a puff. Instead, he placed his elbows on the table, holding his head in his hands with the cigarette held in his right. He studied John's face far too long, before the silence was broken by the squawk of the parrot saying, "Ana." The man didn't flinch. He was deep in thought. I could see the wheels turning in his head as his eyes moved back and forth.

"You know, it's an interesting thing, these dreams. It can be a beautiful thing. Take you and this . . . Madam, for example. She's a married woman who can escape her life at night and have her fantasy with you until the waking hour. She does it alone, without the trouble of having to bring anyone with her. You know, her kids, her mother, her mother-in-law, and most importantly, her husband. You see, Mr. Randall, when the dream is all done, your friend can go back to her life as if . . . ." He shrugged his shoulders. "As if nothing was wrong. She would never have to admit guilt. Too bad it doesn't last forever, though. You know that.

"You never answered my question."

"What question was that?"

"What happened to Ana?"

"Oh, she got what she wanted."

"I see?"

The man with the monocle checked his wristwatch.

"You'd better get going. Madam will be drifting away soon."

John stood up and reach for the door handle, before turning back to face the man.

"Oh. I'll need some wood."

Chapter 7: Fire and Heat

After John lit the fireplace, Mary removed her coat and lay on the floor, taking in the warmth from the fire. Fire was mutually beneficial to John and Mary while she was in her dream-escape. For her, it satisfied her mood and of course provided her comfort. For John, it decreased his desire to steal her body heat and relaxed him, like a sort of sedative.

"Come closer," Mary said, raising her hand to his face. "You're not as cold now," she said stroking his cheek. "You know, I think of you often in my waking life. Your caring nature and your handsome face, get me through the day."

John lay silent, letting her enjoy her dream.

"If I could be honest with you, my day revolves around falling asleep; falling asleep and then arriving in this . . . this world to meet you. I now live for nighttime. Strange, but I like it."

John lay there in his sedated state, taking in the gentle touch of her hand as her eyes scanned his body up and down as she caressed it. He let his eyes close as he was enjoying the touch. He could feel Mary's kisses on his cheek and lips, which worried him.

"Just do that," he said. "Caress me, please."

As the fire roared, the two lay on the floor, inches away from each other. John was indeed feeling intoxicated by the heat and the petting. It was satisfying for him to not have to crave her heat. He knew he would have to eventually, but not that night.

*   *   *

The fire had gone out, and morning had broken. Mary was long gone, and once again, John felt empty. Fire was a drug for him, but it was different than body heat, as he craved it much like a conscious person would crave sex. Fire was addictive and expensive.

John spent the morning thinking of Mary. He felt confused when she came to mind. He wanted her heat, which worried him. It worried him because he didn't know if he could control it once he got a taste of it. When he wasn't thinking about it, he thought about her romantically, which caught him by surprise. His thoughts then changed to Ana and what the man with the monocle had said. Ana was like him, a thief. He knew he was going to commit the act, when the right time presented itself. He felt shame thinking of it. *I wonder if Ana felt shame for carrying out the deed.*

Several nights went by and no Mary. John had strolled up and down the street, keeping his eye on the bench as he walked past it. He even sat on the bench for hours at a time until five nights later, she finally arrived. She entered John's apartment, beaming with excitement.

"Look! I got you something," she said, passing John a small parcel. She started to take her coat off but stopped.

"No fire?"

John needed to lie.

"I'm . . . I'm out of wood, sorry. You didn't come the last few nights. I used it up."

"Oh. That's a shame," she said shoving her coat back over her shoulders. "I'm sure I'll figure a way to warm up," she said as she took her seat. "Open it!"

John unwrapped the box and untied the bright red bow. He recognized the paper. He pulled out a long scarf.

"It's linen. It's all they had at the cute shop across from where we met. It's such a lovely street, the way the lights turn on, just as I arrive. Very charming."

"Thank you, my dear," John replied, wrapping the scarf around his neck, taking in its familiar aroma. "What do you think?" He stood in front of her, who stared off into the distance for a moment before her eyes finally reconnected with John's. "What's wrong?"

"Oh . . . nothing. Just a funny little flashback."

John recalled Arthur's flashback and wondered if he entered one of Mary's dreams earlier on too.

"Care to share the thought?" John took his seat across from her.

"It was a dream I had. I just realized it was you. The flashback was of you throwing the scarf around your neck and saying, 'thank you, my dear.'"

John didn't respond. He knew that it was all working, as he had her where he wanted her. While he sat there, he wasn't looking at her beauty, body language, or the way she was soaking him in. He was looking at the partially open coat, craving the heat that was hidden underneath her coat and her clothing.

"You've got quite the mischievous look on your face. What exactly are you thinking, Mr. Randall? What's going on over there?"

John had trouble controlling himself, so he bolted out of his chair quickly, unwrapped the scarf from around his neck. He held it up high, scanning its length and grinned when he noticed it had an extra piece hanging from it.

"I just had a thought," John said as he brought the scarf to the kitchen. Moments later, he arrived in the main room with the scarf in one hand and a small piece of linen in the other.

"Take this with you tonight. Hold it in your hand when you leave my dream and again just before falling asleep the next night. That way, you won't miss a night with me."

"Just like with the money?" Mary asked.

"Exactly!"

"OK, my sweet. I'll try it."

John's plan was working. He was less anxious now as he didn't need to wait until she'd return to his dream. It was all falling into place until Mary got up from her chair and lay on the floor as she had a few nights ago.

"Come, Mr. Randall. Come closer to me."

John hesitated. He felt it as she lay there, her coat spread, inviting him in, like a wide-open door.

"But I'm cold, my dear."

"It's OK. I'll adjust."

John struggled to control his urge. All the scenarios that ran through his mind to delay stealing her heat had all but vanished from his now irrational mind. As he positioned himself beside her, he had one last surge to hold off.

"What's wrong, my sweet?" Mary opened her coat, taking John's cold hands and wrapping them around her waist. She winced as his hands made contact with her body, then let out a breath of relief. "It's OK."

John could feel her warm breath passing by his face. He was too weak to control himself now. He reached his neck out and kissed her wet warm lips. Mary pulled back slightly.

"Finally. I get to kiss you," she said before holding him tighter and re-joining their lips.

John's instinct took over. Bit, by bit he felt her heat transfer to him. He pulled her even tighter while kissing her. Mary was becoming obviously aroused while John was taking advantage of her willingness to have him, but Mary's desire for John didn't last. She became less mobile and their kisses became loose. John felt the transformation happening to him, which took over any ability to think of anything else but to steal every last morsal of heat. As he took it in, he felt like he had a few weeks ago before he met up with Arthur. He recognized the aliveness of his body and mind. The memory of the conscious world was ever-so clear now. He had what he wanted, to be alive again!

John pulled himself away from Mary's cold limp body. He took his seat and stared at her motionless figure, with her arms positioned beside her head from having her pinned down. He was too rejuvenated to feel anything else, so he did what he had been wanting to do for the last two weeks --; to close his eyes and re-enter the conscious world.

The End

Part 2: Searching for Mary

Chapter 1: The Recovery and the Guilt

Saturday, April, 7, 1984 12:31 pm

It had been almost four months since I woke from that dead-dream-like-state, otherwise known in my conscious life as a coma, the coma Arthur put me in when I mistakenly escaped into his dream. I often reminisced about Arthur and Ana, the love Arthur had for her and her betrayal, the rent collecting man with the monocle and of course Mary, the one I betrayed. The guilt I carried with me was heavy, and not a day went by when I didn't think ashamed for what I did. Many times, I tried to convince myself that it wasn't me, that it was someone else, but I was just fooling myself. The guilt became increasingly stronger as time passed and I found it difficult to push it out of my mind.

I became obsessed with how I could get into that dream-escape, give my heat to Mary and deal with the consequences, even though it would mean that I would never come out of a coma. Many ideas floated through my mind, but I couldn't think of a way. None of my dreams brought me back to her, and there was no way of getting back to that specific dream-escape without that piece of linen Arthur took.

Saturday, April 7, 1984 2:05 pm

I edged my way into the driveway of the house where I bought that leather-bound trunk from last summer. I parked my car and made my way to the front steps, took a deep breath and knocked.

"Yes," answered the older woman that I recognized from my day of purchase.

"Hi. I'm sure you don't remember me, but . . ."

The woman stuck her index finger at me with accusation: "You're the young man who bought the trunk! Of course, I remember you."

I opened my mouth to speak but was interrupted again.

"My husband was asking about you."

It was at this point, that I came to the conclusion that the man I read about that was in a coma for almost twenty years was the same man who owned the trunk before I purchased it. *His* name was Arthur. That was no coincidence. This was a very risky move for me to visit him that day, but I had to tie up some lose ends and this was the first of them.

"Oh," I replied, not knowing what else to say without giving it away.

"Come. My husband isn't well, but he'll want to talk to you."

The house had the smell of chicken broth and freshly made toast. The surroundings were very yellowish as the décor hadn't been updated in about thirty years.

"Arthur," the woman called out, stepping away from me, leaving me standing inside the front door. "That young man I told you about is here."

I could hear the voice of a man reply back, but it was too faint to make out what he had said.

"That young man, who bought the chest," she repeated even louder now. "he's here."

"Where?" the man responded.

"He's at the front door."

I tried to make out his voice and his response but couldn't. The woman returned to where she had left me.

"Come in." She peered down at my shoes.

"I'll take my shoes off."

I knelt down to un-do my shoelaces, which when I noticed my hands were shaking. I was certainly nervous as I wasn't sure what was going to happen, but I needed to do this. So many things ran through my mind: *Was Arthur going to recognize me? Does he think I'm after revenge? What could he possibly be thinking?*

The old woman walked me to the main room where an elderly man was sitting in front of a wooden tray, watching the television. On the tray in front of him was a small plate with a piece of half-bitten toast and two bottles of medication. The old man appeared nothing like the Arthur I met. He was thin with hair that looked like tiny white threads, swept across the top of his head. His face was gaunt and hollow, but he still had that angry demeanor in his piercing blue eyes. He studied me while I entered.

"What's your name, boy?" Arthur asked.

"It's . . . it's John," I answered with awkward hesitation.

Arthur turned to his wife. "Please Darlene," he said pointing to the TV. "Do you mind shutting it off? I'll need to talk to this . . . John for a moment."

The old woman shook her head and waddled across the room, as it appeared she had a bad hip. She flicked the television off and left the room. The man gestured to a chair which had a knitted blanket folded on the back, which was obviously his wife's chair.

"Have a seat," he said with a very weak, scratchy voice. "My throat is very sore today," he said pointing to it.

The old man was definitely Arthur, but a much older version of the man I met in the dream-escape. He was no longer the stalky man that wrestled me to the ground. I wasn't sure who would be the first to open the conversation, but I thought it best for it to be him.

"Did my wife tell you? I had been in a coma for almost twenty years?"

"Yes, I heard." I sat there and decided not to divulge anything more. It was like I was on the other end of a chess board, waiting for Arthur to make the first big move. He had a very mean stare, which I recalled from the dream. Even though he was a much different looking man then the one in the dream, he still possessed that hostile demeanor as if he had always got his way and would be determined to get it eventually if at first, he didn't.

"I would like my chest back," Arthur expressed, pinching his eyebrows together, peering across the room at me. "My wife should never have. . ." he let out a cough. "She should never have sold it."

I watched as his wrinkled hand shook, while it rested on the wooden tray. Even though he was still sporting his wicked stare, I needed to negotiate. There was something I wanted.

"I can bring the trunk back later today if you like, but . . ." I said, raising my finger. "I need that piece of linen back." I paused, before finishing. "Fair trade?"

Arthur reached for his glasses that were on the table beside him, fumbling with the arms as he struggled to place them on. He then leaned forward, his eyes watering slightly as he had trouble holding his focus.

"So. It *is* you," he said as he took his glasses off. "How in the hell did you get back?"

"I became a thief too, just like Ana."

Arthur's face tightened up when I mentioned her name. I could tell it still hurt him, just as I did Mary. The wheels in his head were turning.

"Why do you want to go back there?"

I took a moment before answering his question. We were both feeling the effects of being hurt, betrayed and then turning the tables on others. It was apparent how much of a vicious circle this had been for both of us. Having said that, we were both keeping our emotions and motives in check.

"I need to fix something."

"I see." Arthur fell back against his chair as if already exhausted. "I can't give you the piece of linen."

"Why not?"

Arthur turned to the doorway, where his wife exited through earlier.

"I may want to go back one more time myself." Arthur's face changed. His eyebrows weren't knitted together as tightly as they were earlier.

His face relaxed a little as if he were too tired to fight. Fight for what, I wasn't sure.

"How about this: I give you back the trunk today. I keep the box . . . with the piece of linen that you hand over. Once I'm done with it, I'll bring it back to you; the linen and the box."

"What about the other box," he asked, with his face tightening up again.

"You mean the empty one?"

"Yes," Arthur answered as if to try and conceal a grin. "The empty box."

Arthur lit up. He was a very scheming man, which repulsed me when he would half-grin like that. He was a person that probably had very few friends in life, but I needed to seal this deal and get out of this man's sight.

"Agreed!" I stood. "So? Do we have a deal?"

"Deal!" Arthur stuck out his hand to shake mine.

I hesitated just before our hands met. That's when I had a flashback of that awful night in the apartment. Once it kicked in that he was no longer a threat, I took his hand and gave it a firm shake.

It was odd, not having that big trunk sitting at the foot of my bed anymore. But I still had the little wooden box with the linen in it. Arthur made a point of passing me the envelope secretly while his wife was not around for the final exchange. There was no doubt it was the same piece, as the aroma was so strong that when Arthur passed me the envelope containing it, I put it in the box quickly and closed it once home. I rested the box on the side table, leaving it closed until I was mentally ready. I wasn't ready that night.

Chapter 2: Who could that be?

Friday, April 20, 1984 4:01 am

John enters a dream

He studied the images ahead of him but couldn't quite make out what they were at first. They eventually came into focus. They were from footsteps. They were prints of footsteps, as if someone had walked in white paint and kept tracking it into some sort of dark corridor. The footprints were white luminescent tracks that John watched as he moved forward. When they stopped moving, so would he. He moved with the prints through the dark corridor until it opened up into a large room with a high ceiling, angled at the top, forming a peak. On one side of the large open room were stained-glass windows, emitting enough light for him to scan the virtually empty space. It was barren with the exception of one bench at the far end of the room, beside a doorway.

As he followed those white footsteps, the silhouette of a woman appeared to be sitting on the bench. The closer he was to the bench, the more vivid the details of her shape, her long gray hair and then finally her face. He recognized her. It was the old woman. It was Arthur's wife.

She had lifted her arm and pointed to the door, her face expressionless. He wanted to stop, but the footsteps continued to the doorway and through it. Once he entered, he reached a stairwell, which he followed as the footsteps were almost getting away from him as they ran down the flights of stairs until they reach another doorway. They took him to another corridor. The footsteps were barely visible as they were clouded by plumes of smoke. He pushed the air with his arms, trying to follow where the steps were taking him. He lost sight of them briefly.

The smoke was getting thicker, causing him to feel constraint in his lungs, but the steps continued forward, until they came to an eventual stop. While he waited, he would see puffs of smoke come towards him, before rising to the ceiling of the corridor.

He pushed away the smoke with his arms, so that he could see clearly. He could see something moving in front of him. It was a flash of something, something metal that would twinkle in the light briefly before disappearing. John continued to push the air around frantically, wanting to see what was in front of him. Bit-by-bit, the air would clear until a shiny object that presented itself. It was round, with a silver rim and glass in the middle. The puffs of smoke stopped, allowing him to see that the round metal object was a monocle, which was still in the man's eye.

The man with the monocle produced his toothy grin, sitting in front of a small table, while John stood on the other side. The man still held his grin, squishing the cigarette in his ashtray, allowing him to see clearer. John peered down to see the white footsteps holding still, which meant he was meant to stop. The man with the monocle was holding a box in both hands, which he slid towards him.

"Take this. Remember, everything comes with a price."

The man with the monocle lit up another cigarette, which quickly filled the end of the corridor to the point John couldn't see the man's face anymore, but he could see the footsteps rushing away. He quickened his pace, holding the box tightly in his grip. The footsteps continued down the corridor to another doorway, which led to another stairwell to which the footsteps went further down a flight. At the bottom of the stairwell was one doorway, which led to complete darkness. The steps were clearly illuminated for him, which was a relief.

The footsteps slowed to a stop and then instantly vanished, creating utter darkness. He held the box tight against his chest, circling in a three-hundred-and-sixty-degree movement in hopes of something appearing.

Something did. It was that of someone's breath, exhaling, without a mouth attached to it. John glanced down to see the footsteps reappeared, giving him comfort. The steps moved in the direction of where the breath was emitting, but the mist from the breath disappeared quickly and re-appeared yards away in the completely random direction, until finally, there was a voice.

"You've returned," the familiar voice said from behind him. "You have something very important in that box."

He recognized Mary's voice immediately but didn't answer. He couldn't. He was muted, but he didn't need to speak. He was willing to do whatever Mary had asked of him.

"Open the box. You will notice something."

He opened it and was immediately taken by the sweet familiar odor. He recognized the scent, which gave him pleasure, but his moment of elation was quickly stopped when he felt the sensation of something or someone reaching into the box.

John watched as the white footsteps ran away, not taking him with them. He could hear Mary gasp and then remain silent as if her mouth was suddenly covered. He could see her frightened eyes wide open with fear until they disappeared into the darkness.

John wakes

Friday, April 20, 1984 6:10 am

I woke in panic! *That was not an ordinary dream. Something happened. Something real just happened.*

I reached for the light to turn it on. To my astonishment, the lid of the box was open. The piece of linen was gone!

I ripped off the covers of the bed and searched under the sheets. *Maybe I grabbed it by accident.* After, searching under the sheets and on the floor, I sat on the edge of the bed, reviewing the dream in my head until it hit me.

"Son of a bitch!"

That was Arthur. He took it!

Not only was the piece of Linen gone, Mary was in trouble. Arthur had something to do with it. The empty box that Arthur made a point of asking for, had obvious powers.

*   *   *

Later that morning, I marched over to Arthur's house. My plan was to pay another visit and get that piece of linen back. If need be, I'd threaten to tell his wife about his dream-escape with Ana if it came to that. I was furious!

"Yes," Arthur's wife answered the door, but she had a very unpleasant demeanor. "What is it you want?"

"I'm here to speak with Arthur," I said firmly.

"He's not here. He's back in the hospital. He slipped back into a coma last night. We are very upset."

I stood there, stunned for a moment, not knowing what to say.

"I . . . I see. I'm sorry."

I stepped away from the door, feeling completely defeated.

Chapter 3: Searching for Mary

Tuesday May 8, 1984, 10:11 pm

Almost two weeks went by since Arthur entered my dream and stole that piece of linen. I was still unsure why Arthur would target Mary. She was definitely in trouble and I had to do something. But if Arthur was in a coma, something must have happened to him too.

I procrastinated too long. It was time to get back into my dream-escape somehow. All I had was that empty box, which I had hoped still had some abilities. I decided to fall asleep with the box left open beside me. I need to find Mary.

John enters a dream

John found himself sitting on the bench across the store where Arthur bought the nightgown and Mary the scarf. As he took in the surroundings, he was firmly planted on the bench, not wanting to get off from it. The building where Mary should appear would only be steps away, so he took in the ambiance of the street until he was ready. He continued sitting there, studying the crowd as they weaved in and out of one another.

He eventually got off the bench and headed up the street to that old gray building until he reached the large black metal door. He gave it a pull, but it didn't open. He paused for a moment, studied it, then gave it a more forceful pull until it gave way from the frame. The door was much heavier than he remembered. He scurried up the stairs to the seventh floor until he reached apartment seven-hundred-and eighteen. Before knocking on the door, he leaned towards it, turning his ear slightly to pick up any movement within the apartment. He did this without result so gave the door a rap and stood still, letting out his warm breaths into the cold air of the hallway.

He heard the sweeping sound of steps dragging along the floor on the other side of the door. The lock slid open, exposing a very old Arthur behind the chain sporting his mean stare from the other side of the door.

He knew something was wrong and certainly did not expect to see that miserable old man.

"Where's Mary," John demanded. He was ready to rip the door open but was able to momentarily contain his rage.

"What the hell are you doing in my dream, boy?" Arthur expressed. His eyebrows weren't tight, as they usually were. He was fearful of something. "Get out!"

"I want to know where Mary is. Is she in here?" John quickly scanned the interior of the room the best he could. "Mary," he called.

"She's not here!" Arthur tried to pull the door close, catching John's hand between the door and the frame."

"Argh!" John screeched in pain. He forced his body against the door, ripping the chain off, pushing Arthur to the ground. He scanned the room, walking around its familiar surroundings.

"Get out of here."

John searched every room, but no sign of her.

"She's gone. I gave her my heat," Arthur expressed, still sitting on the floor. "I forced it on her, so she is saved, boy. Now help me up."

Arthur looked up at him, his hand held out. John hovered over him, his warm breath dissipating into the cool air.

"Oh, no you don't. I'm not falling for that again." He slid a chair closer to Arthur, so that he could push himself off it. "Here!"

"Oh. Come on, boy. Help an old man up. It's not you I'm after."

"Who then?"

"Ana." Arthur let out a breath as he was showing fatigue. "She's the reason you and I are in this mess. I risked my life to seek revenge. I'm a dead man anyway. I'm too sick to live a normal life now."

Arthur appeared broken and feeble sitting on the floor.

"Come on, boy. Help an old fool up," he said, reaching his arm towards him.

John stretched out his arm. Arthur's cold hand held his firmly, but not tight. Once Arthur was on his own two feet, he clenched John's hand tighter covering it with his other hand like he did before. To John's surprise, Arthur's grip was quite strong. He pulled Arthur's hands away, causing him to fall on the floor again but did not lose his grip. John panicked, feeling the transfer of heat. He then pushed his full force against Arthur to release his hand, until Arthur finally relented, releasing his grip, his arms falling to either side. Arthur gasped for air.

"What's wrong?"

Arthur pointed to his throat, gasped again, his eyes rolled back into his head. This continued for a few more seconds, until he remained almost motionless. Arthur took one last inhale, before letting out a shallow breath, leaving his mouth open.

John leaned back, his knees still on the floor. He knew that Arthur was dead. He continued kneeling in the same spot until Arthur's body drifted back into his now real-but-dead world.

He bowed his head, contemplating the entire scenario. He considered how reckless the two men were of their own missions resulting in one man's death and one woman's broken heart.

He started to worry about the time, so before he drifted back to his own conscious state, he searched the apartment for that piece of linen. It was easily discovered on the mantel where Arthur must have left it. He didn't want to risk leaving it there, only to fall into someone else's hands, so he tucked it in his palm, sat on the familiar red cushioned chair and drifted off.

Friday May 11, 1984, 1:30pm

I grabbed a local paper like I had every day since my last encounter with Arthur. I quickly flipped through the back of the paper to scan the obituaries and there it was, finally, Arthur Driscoll's death. He died in the early morning of May ninth. I must say, I was relieved to read of his passing. I took a deep breath and let it out, feeling like a huge weight was lifted off my shoulders.

Chapter 4: You Choose

Saturday May 19, 1984, 11:09pm

A week had gone by since my last disastrous dream-escape. I felt unsatisfied by the fact the Mary was saved by Arthur and not me. The guilt of how I treated Mary would not go away as I felt the need to explain to her everything that happened and why I did what I did, but I couldn't think of a way to do that other than risk another dream-escape, but this time, without the fear of Arthur.

There was one thing that could bring me back to Mary and that was the linen scarf. I was too pre-occupied by what transpired that during that last escape for me to think clearly. I was too pre-occupied with that square piece of linen to realize that the scarf might be my ticket back to Mary. But, to get the scarf, meant I had to travel back to that dingy old apartment, using the frail piece of linen that gave me so much trouble to re-acquire.

As soon as I opened the tiny wooden box, that familiar sweet smell reinvigorated the senses, which caused all those memories to come flooding in. I tucked myself under my sheets and placed the linen firmly in my right palm and closed my eyes.

John enters a dream

John found himself on the familiar sidewalk, just outside the shop. He opened the palm of his hand, exposing the piece of frail linen, before shoving it in his pant pocket. It was a cold evening, just as he remembered in Arthur's dream. He wore a wool coat, which he pulled tightly to keep warm. Snowflakes fell from the night sky, which hovered in the air, one by one until they dropped onto his shoulders. He stopped for a moment, peaked in the shop, before his dream-escape led him to his next position. He knew where he was going to go next. The dream-escape was extremely vivid. He didn't even have to think about what to do next.

He pulled the lapel of his coat tight across his open neck to shield the cold. The snow landed on his face as he maneuvered through the sidewalk and eventually towards the old gray building, finally reaching for that all-too-familiar large metal door.

He navigated through the hallways and stairwells until he reached the seventh floor. A few steps further and there he was, in front of door seven-hundred-and eighteen. He took a deep breath in before knocking. He waited for a moment until he heard shuffling on the other side of the door, which troubled him. *Has Arthur returned?*

The door opened slowly exposing a familiar face. It was Ana.

"Yes?" She asked quietly.

"I . . ." John hesitated as he was lost for words. He knew the woman as Ana from living through Arthur's dreams, but she wouldn't have known who *he* was. She glanced up at him with her beautiful gray eyes. It was at that instant that he felt it. He felt the lure of her, but he knew what she was capable of. He needed to get into that apartment, one way or another. "I'm looking for someone."

"Who?"

"A woman . . . named Mary," he replied, his warm breath penetrating the air between the two.

Ana didn't answer right away. Instead, she studied him for a moment before eventually smiling. "I don't know anyone by that name. You must be cold. What is your name?"

"John. John Randall."

She closed the door slightly, unlatched the lock to open the door all the way. "Nice to meet you. I'm Ana. Come," she said, tilting her head towards the inside of the apartment, signaling him to enter."

John stood in the hallway for a moment, however, his need to be cautious diminished. He was losing control of his ability to manage his purpose.

"Come in. Don't be shy."

He let his guard down and he knew it as soon as he passed through the doorway. Ana re-latched the door.

"Please. Have a seat," she motioned to him as she sat in the red cushioned chair that he had seen her in so many times before. John scanned the apartment, taking in its familiarity: the mantel, the clock and the unlit fireplace. He was unsure why she would be here as she already stole Arthur's heat, but he could sense she was a cold soul again, for whatever reason.

"I'm sorry. I don't have any wood, otherwise I'd light a fire for you." Ana wore a red robe that was tightly closed shut with its belt.

"That's OK. I'll keep my coat on."

"What led you here?" she asked.

John had to be quick with his reply. He was dealing with a dangerous dream-persona, but he had trouble focusing on his true motive, finding Mary.

"I don't know. I'm just following my dream." He knew he had to be creative. "But I'm glad I found you."

"Me too," she let out a smile, pulling up her feet, wrapping her arms around them.

Ana held his gaze. It was as if she was purposefully mesmerizing him with them. It was working because he felt an intense desire to be with her. He lost all sense of caution. Mary became a distant memory as John was now lost in his dream. He hadn't a care what would happen to him next.

She got off her chair and knelt in front of him, placing her hands on his knees. He felt how cold she was, but he didn't want her to stop. It took everything for him to not take her hand in his. His feeling of danger was mixed with desire.

"You like me, don't you?" she asked.

"Yes." He was now completely vulnerable. "I want you."

John was already starting to drift.

"I want you too," Ana expressed. "Will you come back tomorrow. Can you hear me?"

"Yes."

John wakes

Sunday May 20, 1984, 5:41am

I woke from my sleep, dripping wet from sweat. I pulled my sheet down to feel my knee where Ana had placed her hand. I could still sense the cold spot where she had placed it.

I closed my eyes to recount the dream, placing my hand on my forehead.

"What the hell was I thinking!"

*   *   *

2:04pm

I finished dotting down notes about my dream with Ana, throwing the pen on the pad as I was disappointed in my behavior. *Have I fallen for her? Or was she luring me in?* When I thought about the dreams I entered as Arthur, I began to take on a different outlook. My feeling towards him began to change because I was never able to completely understand the decisions that he made regarding Ana, and I had hated the man, but now, I empathized with him.

Even though I was angry with myself with how I behaved the night before, there was something pushing me to visit her again.

Friday May 25, 1984, 11:03pm

The week went by and I couldn't think of anything else but to enter into another dream-escape with Ana. I was going to enter the dream and do my best to manage myself, but this time, I brought money proactively.

There I was, in bed, clutching fifty dollars in one hand and the piece of linen in the other.

John enters a dream

Once he focused, the dimly lit shop was in his direct view. He sat calmly, watching the pedestrians rush back and forth along the sidewalk. The streetlamps lit up along the sidewalk, one by one, which illuminated the specks of snow that fell from the dark sky. He took in the cool night air before letting out a long exhale, eventually pushing himself off the bench and heading towards the apartment.

Once in the building, he gave the door a knock as he would have seen Arthur act out so many times. He was very focused that night. He needed to be with Ana. He wanted her.

"Hello, Mr. Randall," she said as she opened the door.

"Hi, Ana." John took his seat on the familiar red chair and glanced down at the un-lit fireplace. "I have a surprise for you."

"Look at you. Presenting a woman with a gift already. I love surprises, by the way," she said with a giddy tone, settling in her seat.

"Well . . ." He broke away for a moment as he reached into his pocket. "I brought money for wood."

Ana's face became almost expressionless as he presented the cash.

"Why would you bring that?"

"To buy wood."

"From where?" She tilted her head slightly. "What makes you think we can buy wood?" Her brow furrowed, causing him to straighten up in his chair. His mouth opened slightly, but he quickly shut it, realizing he may have given himself away.

She stood from her chair, her expression cold and calculating. She leaned towards him, taking in a sniff.

"I recognize that odor. You're hiding something."

"What do you mean?" John stuffed the bills back into his pocket. He was beginning to regret entering his dream-escape. It took everything for him, not to jump out of his chair and run for the door, but he decided to play it cool. "What? What odor."

Ana's eye suddenly widened.

"You're an imposter!"

He got out of his chair and made for the door.

"You're . . . you're crazy! I don't know what you're talking about," John placed his hand on the chain to unlatch the door but stopped when he felt her cold hand on the back of his neck. "Stop it. You thief!" He pushed her away, she bounced against the back of the red chair, then regained her balance. "Stay away from me."

John held out his left arm, while he blindly unlatched the door with his right. He felt instantly exhausted from the loss of heat.

"You realize that if I touch you one more time. . . you're a dead man."

His breathing didn't slow. He knew she was right. One more tight grip from her and he's back in a dead-dream state.

"Give me the linen," she demanded.

"Why?" He was almost out of breath, panting as if he just ran a mile.

"Because . . .because it's mine. *You're* the thief!" She presented a devilish grin. "Besides . . . I have something you may want. It was left here.

Perhaps it was from this. . . Mary woman you asked about.

"What is it?"

"A scarf."

"Let me have it." John's back faced the door. "Put it on that table and back away."

Ana didn't move, causing him to back up and place his hand on the doorknob, not letting her out of his sight.

She screwed her mouth to one side, turning to the dresser behind her, opening the top drawer, finally producing the linen scarf. "Come and get it."

"Nice try. No. On the table or I'm leaving." John turned the handle. "Why are you back here, anyway," He asked. "You already stole Arthur's heat."

Ana laughed: "Because I'm a sucker for love, just like . . ." she peered down at the scarf that was clenched in her hand. ". . . just like your lover, Mary. You must have broken her heart."

He rushed over to grab the scarf, which she quickly hid behind her back, backing away from him at the same time.

"Ah ha. A brave one, aren't you?"

"Give it to me!"

He became increasingly closer to Ana who kept the scarf behind her back, while peering up at him, cracking a smirk.

"You're going to have to wrestle me for it."

"I'm not in the mood for games."

"So . . ." Ana said as she was pressed against the window. "It wasn't me you wanted all this time."

"I told you when we first met that I was searching for Mary, but . . ." John reached for the scarf, missing it as she continued to twist and squirm away, laughing as she did. "But you told me you hadn't heard of her."

"That's because I thought you were handsome."

He placed his hands on her arms, with the intent of holding her still, but the coolness prompted him to immediately release.

"You liked that didn't you? You want to touch me, don't you?"

"Oh, no you don't! You're not going to steal my heat like you did Arthur's."

"That wasn't on purpose." Ana was clearly upset by his comment. "Besides. Who are *you* to talk!"

He was stopped by the accusation which definitely hit a raw nerve. He scanned the floor where he left Mary.

"No. I suppose not."

John reached in his pocket to retrieve the yellow linen.

"Take it." He held the piece of frayed material in his palm. "I have no use for it and Mary will probably never forgive me. Take it and I'll be on my way."

Ana reached for the piece, placing it between her index finger and thumb. John turned to the door and opened it before taking one last glance back.

"If . . . for some reason you meet Mary, you know . . . since you have the scarf. Tell her I'm sorry. I wanted to find a way to . . . ahh. . . never mind." He waved his hand in defeat and walked out the door.

"John," Ana called.

He stopped: "Yes."

"I think you're a good man. I wish you would stay."

"It's dangerous. You know that. I'll always be worried you'll take my heat. And even if you don't plan on it. And . . . well, as I remember it: one can't control oneself. . . can they?"

"Here!" She held out the yellowed piece of linen.

"Why are you giving this back to me?"

"Because. Maybe you will visit me. In your dreams."

He tilted his head to once side, taking in this new side of her. He was still suspicious, but he didn't completely rule out the fact that it may be a genuine side of her, so he plucked the fabric out of her hand.

"OK." John grinned and turned to the door. "I wish there was a way we could remove the threat."

"I agree." She glanced at the mantel clock. "It's quarter to five. You still have time. Where will you go? Why don't you stay."

He pushed the piece of linen in his pocket. "I need to clear my head. It's best I leave." John paused. "I don't suppose you'll give me that scarf."

Ana pulled the scarf from behind her back, peering down at it.

"If you want the scarf, you need to exchange it for my linen. You can't have both. You choose: either me or Mary."

He reached into his pocket but didn't take his hand out. Instead, he removed it to pull the door open.

"Good night, Ana."

The door closed behind him as he strode through the dirty hallway of the apartment.

John wakes

Saturday May 26, 1984, 6:38am

I un-clasped my palm to see the very frail piece of yellowed linen. I brought the palm of my hand to my nose to take in a whiff before placing it in the box and closing it.

3:01 pm

I was edgy all day. I questioned myself about why I took Ana's linen verses Mary's scarf, but I also knew that there was no guaranteed way back to Mary even with the scarf. Having said that, I still wanted to explain myself to Mary. I wasn't convinced that was such a good idea either. Besides, she was a married woman in her waking life. Arthur saved her. *I suppose I'll just have to accept that and not become the hero I had hoped to be, but now, what about Ana?* Was she genuine in her offer? She didn't force herself on me, but that could change in a second. Think, John, think!

Sunday May 27, 1984, 11:02pm

I needed a day to think things over, and, although I came to no final resolution, I ultimately wanted to see Ana, so another dream-escape it was. I placed the linen in my hand, clenching it in my fist as if determined that it will produce a positive outcome. I was very reckless with my emotions that night. I could have stopped this whole thing and be done with it, but I was addicted to it and I wanted her. I was well aware of the danger that it presented.

John enters a dream

He became anxious upon hearing the latch release, but the face that appeared wasn't Ana's.

"Mary!" He said from the hallway.

"Hello, John." Mary was nearly without expression until the edges of her lips raised. She shut the door partially, unlatching the chain. "Come in."

He stood at the entrance, still astonished by how surreal this all was. Mary stood a few feet away, wearing a green dress, her bare arms exposed. She peered down at the floor for a moment, fidgeting with her fingers.

"How did you . . ." Before he could even finish his sentence, Mary ran to embrace him. "What happened? You're like an iceberg."

Mary's face became somber.

"I will explain."

"There are many things I have to say to you too."
He took his usual seat. "I didn't mean to take your
heat. Something took me over and I . . ."

She raised her hand as to hush him. "I never
blamed you."

"How . . ." John started. ". . . how did you get
back?"

"I wanted to see you. . . one last time. I kept the
piece of linen you cut for me, so when I entered
my dream, I found a woman named Ana. She
explained everything to me. I agreed to exchange
heat with her, so that I could be here when you
arrived."

"You what? Why?"

"Because. She said she will return the next night
and we will. . . make the exchange."

He hesitated, wondering why she would be so
trusting of her.

"You know . . ." Mary continued. "I really wanted
to be with you. You hurt me when you left."

"I know. I'm not proud of myself."

Still in her chair, Mary leaned forward placing her
cold hand on his knee: "I believe you."

He studied her hand as it rested there. He took a chance and placed his hand over top of hers, feeling the transfer of heat begin to take place.

"I miss what we had, my sweet," Mary said, not removing her hand.

John sat silent, recollecting everything that had happened between the two and the journey it took to finally meet up with her. He longed to settle things with Mary but had fallen for Ana in the process. He was torn between the two women and hadn't planned for the event where he would have to choose. His dream-escape-state would not let him think rationally, so rather than force an outcome, he let the dream play out on its own.

"John," Mary said, gazing up at him.

"Yes."

"This dream won't last much longer. Will you kiss me one last time?"

"Yes. I want it. I want to kiss you." He surprised himself with his lack of hesitation.

He braced himself when she stood and leaned towards him, placing her cold lips on his. The kiss was a hard, fully-pressed kiss. He could feel the heat transfer immediately, but he didn't fight it.

He just let himself lose consciousness, drifting into that all too familiar dead-dream-like state.

Chapter 5: One could always use a friend

John could feel the warmth of the sharp bright light that peaked through the blinds, creating a horizontal beam that ran across the right side of his face causing him to wake. He slowly leaned forward, feeling woozy as if he were waking from a hang-over. He squinted, trying to focus on his surroundings.

"Mary?" He called out, but there was no response.

He placed his hand in front of his mouth, exhaling his cold breath upon it. He fell back into his chair.

"You're such a dammed fool."

*   *   *

He knew the routine all too well. He would stay and rest during the daylight hours and would search for heat during the night. But it wasn't just that: he became a different man when he was stuck in his dream. He was like a wild animal stuck in his cage during the day: pacing it like a tiger would in its cage. He was impatient with how long it would take before nightfall, which was the only time he could enter the evening's atmosphere.

Once the night sky had fallen, John wasted no time. He roamed the busy sidewalk in search of heat. Hours went by and not one heat source, not one person, male or female, emitted a misty cloud of warm breath into the air. He continued strolling up and down the sidewalk relentlessly until the beginning of daybreak. The little bit of sun would already sting his eyes, so he quickly retreated to the apartment to seek protection from the sun's rays.

As each night passed, he lost hope with the fact that he would ever find someone to steal their heat. He needed to get out of this jam and there was only one other person that could help him.

*   *   *

He positioned himself in front of apartment one-hundred-and-one. He could smell the all-too-familiar cigarette smoke seep through the crack of the door.

He heard the door unlatch, before it opened. The man with the monocle flashed his crooked grin. He pointed at John before speaking: "I knew you would be coming to see me," the man turned to take his seat at the kitchen table.

He stood at the door, surprised by the man's foresight.

"Come in," the man with the monocle said. "We have much to discuss."

"Do we?" he asked, reaching for the back of the chair.

"Dead man," screeched the parrot, causing John to jump as he had forgotten about the annoying bird.

"You'll have to excuse him. He can be . . . how shall I say . . . inconsiderate."

The parrot continued to make clicking noises after it's outburst which he found difficult to ignore.

"You were victimized once again," the man said lighting a cigarette. "Excuse me. Would you like . . ." the man asked, offering his box.

"No, thank you."

The man with the monocle exhaled his smoke into the air.

"I'm curious," the man started, raising his one eyebrow as he readied himself to ask a question. "What brought you back?"

"I was hoping to find someone. A woman. Her name is . . . Mary." The man with the monocle waited for John to continue. "You see. I stole her heat. I couldn't help it. I really liked her. I was ashamed for what I did."

"I see." The man took a long drag, squinting as he did.

"I came back here, using Arthur's dream-piece, but instead of finding Mary, I discovered Ana. I lost myself and . . . well, when I returned to see her, Mary appeared and . . . you know the rest."

The man nodded his head and studied his fingernails.

"Can you help me?" John pleaded; his hands held tightly together between his knees.

"Mr. Randall," the man said with his French accent, sliding his hand along his greasy black hair. "I am very limited." The man turned away from him, rubbing the back of his neck before straightening up in his chair. "You need to find another live one. You know, to . . . steal their heat."

"I don't want to do that again. It's a vicious circle."

The man nonchalantly nodded, not making eye contact with John, but continued to study his fingers and fingernails.

"Where you in love?" the man asked.

"Yes."

"With . . . if you don't mind me asking . . . with which one?"

"What do you mean?"

"With which woman were you in love with?"

He thought to himself before answering: "Mary. I was in love with her. In the end, she took my heat and left me like I did her. I deserved what I got.

"And Ana?"

"Why all the questions?" he asked, bursting in frustration.

"Monsieur. Don't be upset with me. I'm just trying to help," the man said with his hand held in front of him, his cigarette bobbing in between his lips as he spoke.

"I never really trusted Ana, but . . . she never betrayed me either." John wrinkled his forehead. "Why? Is there something I should know?"

"Aye . . ." the man with the monocle turned away, gritting his teeth as he did. "Ana, is a sort of . . . different woman. . . unlike the others, she has her own sort of . . . let's just say. . . abilities."

"Meaning?"

"Aaaannnaaa," called the parrot.

After the parrot's interruption, the man with the monocle grinned his sly grin, while peering down at the table.

"Perhaps there is another way." The man with the monocle finally made eye contact with his guest.

He leaned in: "Yes. Go on."

"Sometimes when I need good luck, I turn to an old friend." Shortly after he expressed this, each of his yellow-crooked teeth emerged from his thin lips.

John shrugged his shoulders. "What do you mean . . . exactly?"

The man with the monocle tilted his head to his left and behind him. "Take Gabriel to your

apartment. Besides . . . he doesn't like my smoke."
He turned to face the bird. "Do you, old friend?"

The parrot let out a fake cough-like imitation and
whistled.

"No thank you. That thing will drive me nuts!"

The man stood, grabbing a cloth material, placing
it over the cage and un-hooking it.

"Here. You can't pay rent while you'll stay here,
so this is your . . . payment . . . if you will."

John took the cage in one hand and steadied the
bottom of it in the other. "If you say so."

"You will need to be patient my friend. Bring him
back in . . ." he made a couple of clicking sounds
with his tongue. "Two days. Leave the cover on
during the daytime."

"OK," he said heading towards the door.

"Au revoir, monsieur," the man with the monocle
said, reaching for the door.

Chapter 6: Stuck with Gabriel

John placed the cage on the dining room table, removing the cover, exposing the large creature.

Gabriel was a blue-and-yellow macaw parrot. He had a long tail and zebra-like stripes around his eyes. John watched as he would open his mouth, appearing as if he wanted to speak, but would produce clicking noises and twist his head around.

"Well. I guess it's just you and me." He peered at the bird as he took his seat in the red cushioned chair.

The parrot was visibly agitated by the absence of its owner. Its movements were erratic, its head twisting and turning, raising its left talon, followed by its right, shifting back and forth on its landing.

John glanced at the mantel clock which read just after four in the morning. He peered down at the fireplace before getting up to wind up the clock.

"I should have got wood. Or maybe you don't need any heat."

"Heat," the parrot squawked.

He took his seat once again, peering up at the clock, listening to its ticking which was, once in a while, drowned out by Gabriel's clicking noises and annoying squawks.

He stretched out his legs, leaning back in his chair, closing his eyes, ignoring the birds' intermittent whistles. He sat waiting until daylight which seemed like forever.

"Hello," the parrot called out.

John waited for a moment, hoping the bird would stop.

"Hello, Gabriel," the bird continued.

"Oh no," John said aloud. "I don't need this . . ."

"He's a dead man," the parrot let out a squawk, further irritating him. "Dead man." He continued and them made his clicking noise.

John got off the chair and approached the cage as if to start a fight with a drunk bar patron. "Stop it. Stupid bird." He paced the room before taking his seat, crossing his arms tightly.

The hours passed but he couldn't rest. The clicking and whistling of the bird would wake him from any possibility of resting, even for a minute.

The bird eventually stopped speaking, letting John rest for a couple of hours.

"Bonsoir," Gabriel called as the sun began to poke through the rim of the blinds.

He fetched the cloth to cover the cage.

"Hopefully this shuts you up," he said as he zipped it up.

*   *   *

"Bonjour! Hello," the parrot squawked.

John woke, glancing up at the mantel clock, which read eleven in the evening. He reluctantly strode towards the cage to unwrap the cage of its cover and plopped himself back down on the chair, closing his eyes once again.

In an effort to continue resting, he ignored the bird, hoping it would stop. He finally closed his eyes.

"It's time," the parrot said and whistled.

"Aaaaannnnaaaa," the bird called slowly. "Aaaaannnnaaaa. It's time, Ana."

Rather than strangle the bird, John tried with all his might to ignore the parrot's annoying calls and noises.

"You look beautiful tonight." When the bird spoke the word "beautiful" it was with a French accent.

"Hello, Gabriel," said a familiar voice which caused John's eyes to open suddenly. "Hello John."

"Oh my . . . How. . . did you get here?" He stood.

She was seated across from him, wearing a full-length coat, the bottom of her bare legs exposed.

"Why is Gabriel with you?" Ana said. "Did Monsieur lend him to you." She bopped her right leg over her left knee. "He's a tricky one, isn't he? Tell me . . . what did he say to you about me?"

"Wh . . . what? You mean the bird?"

"No silly. Monsieur. The one with the. . ." Ana motioned her right hand over her eye, creating a circle with her index finger and thumb. ". . . one eye-glass."

"He didn't say. . . anything, really."

"He didn't? I'm surprised . . . and yet again. I'm not."

John was temporarily distracted by her warm breaths that he had difficulty focusing. He quickly regained it, peering over at Gabriel, then back at Ana.

"What's going on? What . . ." John backed towards the door, confused by the circumstance. "What is it with you and that bird?"

Ana laughed: "What? Gabriel? He's the one that brings me back." She stood from the chair and took a step towards John. "As for Monsieur. Let's just say . . . we have a sort of . . . connection."

She continued towards John, sporting a sly grin.

"Tell me . . .Did you meet your love?"

John hesitated before answering, peering down at the floor as if embarrassed: "Yes."

"You're cold, aren't you? Let me guess; she stole your heat."

John nodded.

"Do you feel . . . deceived?"

"No. I deserved it. I knew the risk of seeing her again. I just thought that . . ." John stopped when she had backed him towards the door. "What are you doing?"

Ana placed her hands on his chest. "Hold my hands."

He did, but quickly pulled away.

"Stop it. I don't want to steal it from you."

"Shhhhh," she whispered, pushing herself on his chest again, peering up at him. "Kiss me. Kiss me like you did Mary."

John couldn't resist the request after getting a taste of the warmth from her hands. It was just a matter of time before he craved more, bringing his hands up to her neck, wrapping them around her exposed flesh. The kiss started hard-pressed, but he pulled back just enough to take her top lip into his, tasting her plush lips.

"That was beautiful," Ana's breathy voice expressed as she weakened in his arms.

John steadied her limp body which became increasingly heavier as she lost all strength. Her neck swung back causing her head to follow as he wrapped his arms around her back to lift her to the chair. He watched her shallow breaths enter the stale, cold air.

Ana's legs were so limp and lifeless that her feet were awkwardly positioned, causing her coat to open when she was planted in her chair. He pulled her coat to close it, let out a long sigh before taking his chair and drifting off.

John wakes

Thursday May 31, 1984, 7:14am

I woke from that very long sleep, my mouth and body parched. I opened my palm to witness the very frail piece of linen, which I carefully placed in the box and closed. I staggered down my staircase to take a long gulp of water which I immediately threw back up. I was weak and my head was pounding. I sat at the kitchen table and took small sips of water and nibbled on a Saltine cracker.

7:32pm

Sitting outside on my front porch, I took in the fresh spring air, feeling more alive than ever. I was content with the notes I had made which I shoved away in my drawer, therefore: it was time.

I opened the small wooden box that was placed beside me. I took the yellowed fabric between my thumb and forefinger, holding it to my eye level before flicking the lighter, destroying those dreams of linen forever.

The End

Part 3: The Eyes of

a Marchesa

The Marches Luisa Casati

Introduction:

The Marchesa Luisa Casati was an Italian heiress and muse. She lived from 1881 – 1957. When her father and mother died, the fifteen-year-old Luisa and her older sister Francesca became the wealthiest women in Italy.

Luisa Casati was very shy as a teenager, but eventually overcame it, living an extravagant lifestyle until she racked up a debt of 25 million dollars in 1930. She eventually fled her creditors and traveled to London where she lived the remainder of her life virtually penniless.

She was also a patroness of the arts and sat for many artists. Her most famous portrait is by Welsh painter Augustus John.

This story is about this incredibly eccentric woman and the famous portrait, which is located at the Art Gallery of Ontario in Toronto, Canada.

T.H. Cini

At the Gallery

Friday, July 3, 1987, 4:46pm

One afternoon, while completely bored with life, I decided to visit the Art Gallery of Ontario. I passed through each room of famous paintings from around the world. Some of them massive and some of the pieces quite small. Although I loved the arts, I wasn't familiar with the artists or the artistic periods that I reviewed as I meandered through each exhibit. It was already three o'clock in the afternoon and I hadn't anything to eat since my breakfast at eight in the morning. I'd already spent close to two hours at the art gallery and was thinking that I should get ready to find my way out when I came across a portrait of a woman with bright red hair.

This one definitely caught my attention, so I decided to study the work a little further. The painting was an ordinary portrait; however, the image was that of no ordinary woman. She had flaming hair that would grab one's attention as soon as you would enter that exhibit. But it wasn't just the hair that held one's attention. It was those large eyes of hers. The model posed with her body turned slightly to the left with the dark of her eyes staring at you directly. I made a few steps closer, positioning myself directly in the middle, not able to break contact with the woman in the portrait. I was fascinated by this woman. I continued to hold her gaze. Patrons came and went, but they didn't faze me in the least. I was completely captivated by the portrait, so much so that I eventually lost my balance and almost fainted, placing my hand to the floor to stop myself. I then sat on the floor for a moment to gain my composure and strength.

"Are you OK, sir?" an employee of the gallery asked, scurrying towards me from the other side of the room.

"Yes. Sorry. I just need to sit for a moment."

"Here," the woman said, fetching the chair she had been sitting on, while watching the gallery's patrons.

I sat until I felt more myself. The employee hovered near. After a couple of minutes, I let out a large exhale and stood up.

"Feeling better?" the employee asked.

"Yes. Thanks. Phew! I almost passed out."

"You were staring at that painting for almost half an hour."

"I what?"

"You were standing in the front of the Marchesa for a least half an hour. You didn't even move. I thought you were frozen in time for a moment before you collapsed."

I checked my watch. It read quarter to four. *She's right. I lost complete track of time*.

"I'd better be on my way." I took one last look at the portrait and left the gallery.

Once out of the gallery, I decided to buy a Gyro from a street vendor, which I devoured. I was hungrier than I thought. This gave me the energy I needed to make the trek home, which would take nearly two hours, as I lived east of the city of Toronto. I had to take a streetcar to union station, take the train from union station to Pickering, then take the bus to Whitby.

*   *   *

Once finally home, I spent a little bit of time re-organizing some of my furniture and put up a few pictures before calling it a day. I'd moved to Whitby from Port Perry in June and still hadn't hung all my pictures.

I re-heated the pasta I had the night before. I enjoyed that with a small glass of red wine before reading in bed.

11:05pm

I was able to read until just after eleven in the evening, but could barely stay awake, so I turned and placed Hemmingway's, *The Sun Also Rises*, on the night table, clicked off the lamp and settled in.

Dream # 1 (Marchesa)

As John drifted, his body felt lighter and lighter, almost as if he were hovering above his bed. He visualized floating high above his bed and eventually above his house. His vision began to change from viewing himself to complete darkness. The darkness only lasted for a few moments before a tiny white light emerged from the center of his field of vision. The white light became increasingly brighter, before changing to a neon-like red beam which, continuously changed form. It then changed into a three-dimensional sphere, which became blue and would pulse, replicating that of a heartbeat. Vein-like rods of energy burst out of the continually beating sphere, emitting small bolts of energy, the light glowing brighter, then dimmer as it did.

This continued until the sphere changed once again into two white spots, that morphed again into two dark brown irises and dilated pupils. The eyeballs moved back and forth, as if the person attached to them were moving around the room, watching him. They finally blinked, and from their direction came a female voice.

"Ciao. Vedo Qualcosa. Ariel. Sei tu?"

"I . . . I don't understand. Can you repeat, please?"

"Forse parli francese. Parlez-vous francais?" The woman's voice continued, her eyes moving and blinking, but no other features could be seen.

"I don't speak French, sorry."

"Anglaise? English?"

"Yes. Engllsh."

"Ah. Very well," said the woman's voice with a thick European accent. "You are not an Englishman, are you." Before he could answer, the woman's voice continued. "You are American. No?"

"I am Canadian."

"Ahh. Très bien. I've never met a Canadian before."

John didn't respond right away as he was trying to determine her accent, but before he could reply, she continued.

"I have tried many times to connect with the dead," she said and then mumbled to herself in Italian. "Are you dead?"

"No. I am alive."

"Quite incredible. I am the one who is dead."

"Oh," He replied.

While listening to this woman, he determined her accent to be Italian. She spoke English quite well and made a point of pronouncing every word as precisely as possible.

"Can you see me?" the woman asked.

"I see your eyes, but nothing else."

The lady remained silent, but her eyeballs shifted back and forth. All this was incredibly mysterious to him. He wasn't frightened. He was intrigued.

"Let me touch you. I want to ensure you are not lying. Don't be afraid." He could sense her come closer to him, then suddenly, clenching his bare arm with her hand.

John Wakes

I woke suddenly, bringing my right hand over to my left arm, where I could still feel her touch until it gradually went away.

"What the hell was that?"

I got out of bed and checked my clock. It read 6:10am.

"*Who* the hell was that?"

All the feelings of the past Dream-Escape came flooding in. I wasn't sure if she was after me for my heat or not, but the thought of it must have frightened me enough to wake me out of that state.

I sat up in bed and leaned back against the headboard, thinking about those large almond eyes because of their intense beauty. *Who was that?* I closed my lids and tried to re-imagine them. While I did, I re-created their movement and finally the touch of her hand, which wasn't cold as what I had experienced in my latest Dream-Escape.

*   *   *

The dream occupied my entire day. I couldn't get that voice and shiftiness out of my mind. I had wished that I didn't wake so suddenly from her touch. I definitely wanted more. The memories of the other Dream-Escape came flooding in, which was surprisingly pleasing. There was fear mixed with pleasure, almost like a high someone would get while racing a car, with the risk of death. It was at that point that I felt the addiction of the Dream-Escape and was determined to see that Italian woman in my dreams again, but who was this and how did she end up in my dream so vividly?

It took several hours to find the box that contained the notes from my last venture into a Dream-Escape, but once I did, I re-read all of them. It was inspiring, but nothing resonated with regards to an Italian woman like her, so I started a new page, dated it last night and made my notes.

Once finished, I covered my face to try to imagine the eyes again, when it hit me.

"The painting. The art gallery. Could that be her?"

I was upset with myself when I realized I didn't ask about the painting or the artist.

"Dammit." I glanced at my watch and thought to myself. "I'm going to call."

I found the number for the Art Gallery of Ontario, took the pad and pen from out of the drawer I placed them in earlier and waited for someone to answer.

"Art Gallery of Ontario information," answered the voice of an older woman.

"Hello. I have a question about one of your paintings."

"We have thousands of paintings in the gallery. I'll do my best, but I can't promise you anything. Do you recall the floor or era? Is it modern, fifteenth century? Seventeenth century? That kind of thing?"

"Ummm. I'm not sure. I'm thinking late-eighteen-hundreds to early-nineteen hundreds. The painting is of a portrait of a woman with bright red hair and. . ." I tried to continue but was cut off by the woman on the other end of the phone.

"That's the Marchesa."

"Huh?"

"It's 'The Marchesa Casati' by Augustus John. He is a Welsh painter. That woman has an incredible history."

"One minute. I'm writing this down. Can you repeat the name of the painting again, please? And the artist. Is she Italian by any chance?"

"Indeed, she is. Read up on her. I can't tie up the phone much longer, sir."

I noted the name of the artist and of the woman, thanked the woman on the phone, then hung up.

I couldn't conceal my smile. I was so delighted by this news and the fact that I had a Dream-Escape with a famous dead person.

The library was closed until Monday, so I had no way of looking up this stranger who entered my dreams.

Monday, July 6, 1987, 6:35pm

I was disappointed each morning I woke since the last Saturday morning. Whatever triggered me to meet the Marchesa Friday evening wasn't registering with me enough to travel in my dreams to meet this interesting Italian woman. I wasn't totally discouraged though, as after work, I made a trip to the library and searched the cards for the artist. Once I located Augustus John's book, I discovered a full-page print of the portrait I had seen. I knelt with the pages wide open on my lap. *Ah, yes. That's her.*

"What an extraordinary looking person," I said quietly.

This should help me with my Dream-Escape tonight.

Once home, I opened the biography on the Marchesa Casati and was astonished by the stories of her transformation from a shy young individual to the vibrant eccentric that she ended up being. She was incredibly wealthy, and the stories of her masquerade parties and the guests were very intriguing. I was so fascinated I continued reading until the time she spent in Venice. It was getting to be late in the evening when I started to doze, which was when I decided to study the Marchesa's eyes before drifting off to sleep.

"This would surely bring me back to you tonight."

Tuesday, July 7, 1987, 7:01 am

My alarm woke me from my deep sleep. Once I came to, I was disappointed once again upon wakening and not meeting the Italian woman I had been so infatuated with.

"Dammit!"

I reached for the book that was on the other side of the bed as I must have fallen asleep with the print of her portrait open. I flipped through it to find that specific page.

"Damn! Damn! Damn! How am I going to meet you again?"

Saturday, July 11, 1987, 2:21 pm

The rest of the week passed and I still hadn't dreamt of the Marchesa, so I decided I must make another trip to the gallery in Toronto and study the original portrait. It was my last hope.

I paid for my entrance, obtained a map where the man at the front desk placed a small star at the location where the painting would be. Off I went and quickly navigated through the exhibits, not paying attention to any of them. I continued through each corridor, glancing at the map, which was clutched in my hand until, with my peripheral vision, from the adjoining room, I saw that brightness. I hadn't even entered the room yet and I felt excited and anxious, as if I were about to meet a celebrity. I stood still for a moment, taking her in before entering. *I could sense her watching me. I'm certain of it!*

I continued casually toward the Marchesa; her stare mesmerized me as I entered the room. Once in front, I fell into the same trance-like state I was in the first time I saw her. I lost track of time once again and would only break contact with her briefly to ensure I didn't lose balance and collapse as I did before.

"That's quite the painting," a gentleman with thick-rimmed glasses said as he stood by me.

I glanced at him quickly and nodded as I didn't want to engage in a conversation, but he continued to stand beside me. I could see him glance at me once more.

"She pissed away twenty-five million dollars in her lifetime." I continued to look forward, but could see him studying my face

Unimpressed with his criticism, I continued to stare at the portrait and not respond, with hopes that he'd go away and leave me alone, which he eventually did with a quiet huff to himself before doing so.

At first, I was distracted by the gallery's patrons' entering and exiting, but I eventually held the gaze without feeling the interruption. She wasn't speaking to me, but I was being pulled into her world, and I don't mean her world that was described through her biography, but as in -- I felt I was within her presence. As if I were a guest in one of her elaborately furnished homes. It took me away, which I needed, which I wanted. *Speak to me tonight, Marchesa. I want to be in your reality.* I could almost see the corner of her lip lift, as if to agree with pleasure of my request. I could barely contain myself from smiling.

"Sir."

I turned around to see an employee of the gallery approach me. "Yes."

"We are closing in fifteen minutes." It was an older male employee that addressed me.

I stretched out my left arm to check the time. It was already quarter-to-five.

"Oh," I replied, still surprised how the time flew by so quickly.

I decided to walk to the portrait from the right and then to the left, so that I could create a three-dimensional image of her in my mind before I left.

"Sir."

"Yes. I'm leaving."

"Good night."

11:12pm

It had been a hot day. While getting ready for sleep, I stripped to my boxers and slid under the covers. I made the decision earlier *not* to stare at the portrait in the library book. The image of the original picture was so clear in my mind that I could replicate the brush strokes that made up her features, but in darkness, the fine details of the painting were transformed.

Dream # 2 (Paris – 1919)

As he drifted, the female stood in front of him. She was positioned with her body turned to her right, her right hand clutching her left with her left placed on her hip. John studied her powder-white flesh draped with her cream silk pajamas. Her red lips glistened as if she had just wet them, and then they moved.

"You have returned."

He was too slow to respond, as he was still taking in the stature of this woman who was in total view. She was just how she was in the portrait, except that she was in a large room with large windows. John studied the room and felt as if he were in a different country.

She let her hands off her hip and strode towards him as if on a runway of a fashion show. She was much taller than he expected. She was six-feet-tall.

"Are you not cold," she asked as she neared him. "Take this and put it on."

The Marchesa reached for a robe and handed it to him. He glanced down to see that he only had boxers on.

"Oh my. I didn't realize . . ."

"I don't care. Be as you are. I didn't want you to be cold." She took a seat on the bright green sofa and lit a cigarette that was placed in a holder. She took a long slow drag from it. Her actions were slow and meticulous as if she were in some type of performance. She nonchalantly waved her free hand towards the chair across from her. "Have a seat." Once she exhaled, they held each other's gaze. He was locked into her involuntarily. "You disappeared on me. You don't like when I touch you?"

The Marchesa batted her large lashes and perfectly placed dark shade beneath, enhancing the largeness.

"Do you Canadians not speak? You are incredibly quiet."

"Yes," John finally replied pulling the blue silk robe around his legs. "I . . . I woke when you touched me. I was surprised because . . ."

"Because of what? That I'm dead?"

"I suppose."

The Italian crouched forward, studying him while still holding her cigarette holder. John was bewildered by her. He was intimidated by her beauty and intense gaze. She seemed to hold her emotions to herself. Her eyes were beautiful, but they were also scheming.

"You are alive and I am dead. This is interesting. You see, when I was alive, I was in constant search for the dead, but now . . ." she took a drag and fell back into her sofa, "I am speaking to the living. Yes. Very strange indeed."

The Marchesa let out a devilish grin, exposing her teeth for the first time.

"You don't know who I am, do you." She crossed her legs, holding her cigarette high in the air with her right hand. She tilted her chin downward, awaiting his response.

Although he was prepared to answer the question, her poker-face-stare was that given from a being who would throw a vase at him for answering incorrectly.

"You are the Marchesa Luisa Casati."

His answer seem to please her as she let out a half-smile before taking another puff.

"And you? You are?"

"John. John Randall."

"John Randall," the Marchesa repeated with her Italian accent. "And your title?"

"Title," he inquired.

"Yes. Title. Do you have a title?"

He was taken back by the question. He straighten himself before answering.

"No."

Luisa Casati sat silent, studying him intently as the wheels continued to turn in her head.

"Are you an artist? A dancer?" She took a puff of her cigarette. "A poet."

"No."

John was becoming even more intimidated. She obviously was used to being surrounded by high-class individuals. Even though he had been critical of the upper class in his waking life, he wasn't critical of her. He was fascinated and even though it was his dream, he let her lead it.

"Let's get you into a proper suit. I want to go out." She got up and headed towards the large windows to peer down the streets. "I need a glass of Champagne." John watched as the Marchesa leaned over the window, the bright light showing off the silhouette of her long thin body from underneath her pajama. "Have you got any money?" She asked without turning to face him.

"No."

"Darling. . ." The Marchesa turned and strode past him with elegance as if nothing could ever frazzle her. "Bring some currency with you, next time."

"OK," he replied awkwardly. He watched the Marchesa's cigarette burn in the ashtray beside what looked like a six-inch crystal ball, resting on a wooden holder.

Luisa Casati, took her seat and lifted her cigarette off of the ashtray. "I will wait."

She gave John a look that would cut through anyone that was at the receiving end of it.

"Away you go." She gave a wave of her hand as if to dismiss him.

"But."

"Yes?"

"What city are we in?"

"Paris darling." She exhaled. "Bring francs."

"One more question . . ."

"Sto diventando impaziente."

"Pardon."

"What is your question?"

"What year are . . . are *we* in?"

"It is nineteen-nineteen. The war has ended."

"What," John answered in astonishment.

Lines formed on her forehead as she thought to herself. "How far into the future are you?"

"Nineteen-eighty-seven."

"Questo è incredible."

"Excuse me."

"Never mind. Bring back some French Francs. We will go out and have fun."

She stood up and strolled to a closet at the other end of the room. He was unaware of what she was doing until she approached him with a two-piece suit.

"Try this on."

He studied it briefly before commenting: "It's small."

"I know it is. Try it on."

John removed the silk robe, placing it on the chair. He filled the pants with both legs, followed by the jacket.

His red-headed friend covered her mouth, trying to conceal her laughter.

"It will do. I will have you fitted with another. Bring a few hundred Francs with you, darling."

John quickly removed the clothes and placed them neatly on the hanger. The Marchesa sat still, still holding her cigarette. He knew she wanted him to return to where he came from, but he couldn't just up and leave; he had to drift back into his natural world.

"I will need to stay until I drift off." He took the robe and covered himself with it and took his seat across from her.

A devilish grin came over the Marchesa who quickly stood up, approached him, leaned in front and kissed him.

John Wakes

Sunday, July 12, 1987, 6:03am

"Oh no!" I sat up. "Dammit!"

I could still feel her lips on mine and the sweet smell of her perfume. I was very disappointed in waking at that very moment.

"Did she do that on purpose to make me wake up?"

I almost touched my mouth with my hands, but didn't want to ruin the tingling sensation.

Saturday, July 18, 1987, 12:31pm

The weekdays dragged by for me as I wasn't able to get into Toronto to view the portrait, and I wasn't able to just go into a bank and have money exchanged into antique francs. Instead, I had to withdraw five-hundred dollars of Canadian money, so that I could buy French currency from nineteen-nineteen or earlier; so, there I was, visiting coin-collector after coin-collector in downtown Toronto, so that I could bring as much money to my Dream-Escape as possible.

2:40pm

After spending nearly five-hundred dollars purchasing twenty French francs from that era, I took a trip to the art gallery.

"You've been here before," expressed the man at the ticket counter.

"Yes."

"Why don't you buy a season's pass? It will be worth it for you if you come regularly."

I pondered the thought for a moment and agreed. "Sure."

I strode quickly through the halls of the gallery which was awkward, having so many coins in my pant pockets as I didn't think to bring a nap-sack, so instead, there I was rushing through the exhibits like a madman so that I could get a good hour in front of the portrait. To make matters worse, each coin came in a cardboard insert with sharp corners.

"Hello, again," the gallery employee, who had straight dark brown hair, said and nodded pleasantly. She'd helped me when I fainted upon my first visit.

"Hi."

"I think you've fallen in love with this portrait." She youthfully stepped closer to me and awkwardly smiled.

I stood for a moment, taking in her statement when.

"It's so striking," I replied. "What do you know about the subject who posed?"

The employee turned to look at the portrait alongside me before speaking: "I know very little except that she was wealthy for her day and by the end of her life, was penniless. She had been seen rummaging through garbage in London, looking for artifacts to make herself stylish. Besides that, I don't know anything else. As for the actual portrait, people just love that pose, her style. I mean, who wouldn't?"

Part of me regretted asking, as I preferred to get to know her through my Dream-Escape rather than third-hand knowledge, which was exactly why I stopped reading her biography.

"I'm sure there is much more to know," I replied as if to be defending her.

"Enjoy your visit." She turned and walked towards a group of observers.

10:51pm

I removed each coin from its protective cover one-by-one until I created two neatly stacked columns on my night table. I stripped down to my boxers, sat on the bedside and placed ten coins in each hand firmly, while gently pushing my legs under the sheets.

Dream # 3 (Giovanni)

John drifted high above his comfortable bed, floating high above the roof and eventually into the clouds. The fog-like atmosphere would collect, compromising his vision, which agitated him until it dispersed and his lungs filled with smokey air causing him to cough.

"Bonjour, mon ami," the Marchesa said as she strolled around the small sofa where he lay, puffing on her cigarette. One of the coins rolled out of John's relaxed hands, creating a clink on the floor. "Meravigliosa!" She knelt and picked up the coin, trying to hold back her grin. "You were successful."

He watched as she twirled the coin in one hand and held the long cigarette in her other. He pushed his chin into his chest to see his arms along his side, just as he did when he dozed off.

"Good morning!"

"Nonsense. It's the afternoon here," she replied, her grin gone as quickly as it came.

He sat up and stacked the coins on the tiny table beside the sofa which his friend quickly glanced at. Her reaction was not a positive one.

"That's nothing near the amount I mentioned. Did you not hear me. . ." The Marchesa stopped mid-sentence. "Forgive me, but I don't think 'John' suits you. I shall call you . . ."

He studied her as she continued to pace the room in her cream-colored pajamas, her long neck protruding out of it, accentuating her height.

"I shall call you Giovanni, yes. That's more suitable."

He didn't debate it and actually liked it.

"Giovanni it is!"

"It's settled, then!" She passed the small table of coins. "About the money. There is only twenty or so francs there. You are not a wealthy man, are you?" She let out a sigh and sat across from him.

"No."

She had the incredible ability to hold her body language in check. "We will make do with what we have."

"How should I address you?"

"Scusi?"

"What should I call you? You will call me Giovanni. What should I call you?"

"You will call me Marchesa." She pushed herself off her chair, moderately annoyed by the question. "Come!" She extinguished her cigarette and continued to the back of the room. "Let's get dressed. We need to get you something to wear."

John turned to follow her when she disappeared behind a folding screen. He watched as her long arms reached high above the screen until her pajama were flung over it.

"Put that suit on, Giovanni. We will get it altered; then, let's go for a nice stroll."

John was happy upon hearing his new European name. He pulled out the ridiculously small suit. He made his way into it, which was uncomfortably tight and he took his seat on the sofa, waiting for her to finish.

She eventually came out from behind the screen wearing a long black dress with a string of pearls that reached her knees. He followed her movement towards the mirror. She adjusted her hair and then applied kohl using the tip of her pinky finger. Once done, she grabbed her shoes, took her seat, strapped them on and quickly stood.

"Let's go!"

John sat still scanning her long body, which appeared even taller with the addition of her heels. The touch more of the kohl around the bottom lashes added an intensity. He was mesmerized by her, not moving an inch, save the bottom of his jaw, which dropped.

"You look absolutely beautiful."

She reached out her black laced gloved hand. "Thank you, darling. Let's go before we lose the afternoon sun."

She slid the money into her small purse and headed for the door. As he continued down the dark hallway, John was anxious and excited about entering 1919 Paris.

Once out, he stopped and gave a 360-degree view of the city and its streets. The roads were dry with dirt, which kicked up dust every time a motor vehicle or horse and carriage would drive by. The citizens of the city were dressed in period clothes, which took him a while to soak in as he knew his Dream-Escape brought him into the realistic Paris of that era.

"Come. The tailor is just down the street. We don't need a cab."

As John walked beside her, his self-consciousness regarding wearing his under-sized suit subsided as his companion was getting all the attention.

Men and women stared at this incredible woman. Her live friend was in awe of her confidence and ability to not be shaken by the on-lookers, their gawks and mumbles under their breaths.

Within two blocks, she stopped in front of the door of the tailor.

"Here we are," she said, holding her purse firmly. She stood beside the door for a moment, before John reached for the handle to open it for her. A stout man with thin black hair and glasses came from around the counter.

"Bonjour mademoiselle."

"Bonjour."

"Comment puis-je vous aider?"

The Marchesa turned to John, pointing at his suit: "Est-ce que je peux. Mon invité ne parle que l'anglais. Can anything be done with this?"

"Monsieur." The man greeted John and approached him pulling the sleeves of the jacket downwards.

"Non," he said, then shook his head. "This is too small. It looks . . ." the man turned to face the Marchesa. "Ridiculous!"

"How soon can you have him in something, fashionable. We need it quickly. We want to enjoy the afternoon."

"Ahhhh," the Frenchman said. "I can have something tomorrow."

"Maintenant, qui est ridicule?"

"Mademoiselle," the Frenchman replied.

"Tout de suite! S'il vous plaît. You have no one in your shop." the Marchesa raised her hand to the air, shrugging her shoulders in disbelief of his answer.

"Very well."

*   *   *

The two waited at a nearby café, while the tailor prepared his new suit. John was almost overwhelmed by his new atmosphere and couldn't stop people-watching. Although the Marchesa was quiet while he took in this new landscape, he noticed her studying him.

"Giovanni."

"Yes."

"How old are you?"

"Twenty-seven."

She looked away briefly, as if pre-occupied by something on her mind before turning to answer.

"We are of the same age," she blurted. "I am twenty-nine." She quickly changed the subject. "Do you have a woman in your life?"

"I had, yes. But not anymore."

"You loved her, didn't you?" She grinned in delight as if catching her guest by surprise.

"I had strong feelings for her."

"Oh, darling. You can't even say it, can you?"

"Say what?"

"That you were in love."

"Have you ever been in love?"

The Marchesa Luisa Casati held her coffee cup in front of her lips, piercingly looking at John's as if he'd committed an awful sin. "I prefer not to talk about it. After all, that is in the past. Need I remind you. I am not a living soul. I am the one who is dead."

John was saddened by the reminder that she was in his dream and technically dead for thirty years.

"You are alive to me."

She took a sip.

"Shall we try something?"

"What is that?"

"Let me touch your hand. I'd like for you to . . . not become awake when we touch."

John hesitated as he didn't want to wake from this wonderful experience, but he was equally interested in the physical contact with her.

"Yes." He paused. "But not yet. Can we wait until after? I don't want to leave. I'm enjoying this."

"Yes, darling." She put her cup on the table and turned to the waiter behind her. "Garçon, l'heure??"

A portly man adjacent to the couple pulled out his pocket watch: "Quatre heures et quart."

"Merci." She turned to John. "Your suit will be ready. Let's pay a visit to the tailor."

*   *   *

The Marchesa paid the tailor who studied one of the coins for a moment, flipping it within his fingertips. John became worried that there would be a problem.

"What is the matter?" He asked.

"Nothing. The coin, it's . . ."

"What is wrong with the coin, monsieur?"

"It is dated this year, but . . . it looks . . . old and faded."

Luisa Marchesa grabbed John's arm and pulled him towards the door.

"Come, Giovanni. I'm in the mood for some caviar and champagne."

Luisa ordered a cab to a restaurant that she said she had been to in the past.

*   *   *

The Marchesa ordered a bottle of champagne and caviar, which disturbed John, as all these were purchased within a matter of hours. His friend was in control of the money, which was almost half gone.

"Something the matter," she asked after the waiter left the table.

John sat quietly before answering. He was torn as he didn't want to bring up money and ruin the mood, but he was afraid of how much money was flying out of her hands. Having said that, he was living this wonderful experience. He stopped himself from confessing what was really on his mind.

"I've never had caviar before."

"Oh, darling. It's incredible. You don't know what you've been missing."

To John, the taste of caviar wasn't exactly nice, but he didn't hate it either. He would wash the taste down with champagne which ended up relaxing him from whatever anxiety he was having earlier.

"Tell me." The Marchesa said, not finishing her sentence until she took a sip from her glass. "How did you find me?

"I don't know what you mean."

"You found me. In your dream. How did it come that you found me?"

"Oh. It was a portrait of you, in a gallery. In Toronto."

"In Toronto, why is my portrait in Toronto? America I can understand, but I have had no connections in Canada."

John shrugged his shoulders. She seemed upset by the news.

"What did the portrait look like? Who's the painter? I need to know his name," the Marchesa demanded, raising her voice causing other patrons to turn and stare at the couple.

Luisa fixated on John. His anxiety increased as she was clearly disappointed with the news. He sat up to ready himself before he answered.

"Augustus John."

"He was a good man." Her thoughts were still brewing. "Which one?"

"What do you mean?"

"Dammit!" The Marchesa slapped her hand on the table with frustration, stopping every conversation on the outdoor patio of the restaurant. "Pardon." She raised her long hand into the air.

"Per l'amor di Dio uomo." Luisa Casati said, leaning towards her anxious guest, her gaze once again cutting through him. "He painted me twice. What did the painting look like? Describe it to me."

John was now upset and embarrassed. He had never seen this side of her before and certainly didn't enjoy it. He scanned the patrons on either side of the table who were talking about them in a low rumble.

"Giovanni. Look at me." The Marchesa softened her tone a little and softened her expression so it was no longer as intense.

"You seemed . . ." he started.

"Continue."

"You appeared as you did when I met you. The second time. When I could see all of you."

"Yes."

"You were wearing your cream pajamas."

"And."

"The background was like. It was like a dark mountainous background."

The Marchesa let out a half-smile and fell back in her chair: "That pleases me. Although . . ." she paused. " . . . I don't understand how my painting made it across the ocean to Canada."

She stared off into the distance, taking in the new information. Although John was still uncomfortable with her sudden outburst, he was relieved that she seemed to be at peace with the outcome.

He raised his champagne glass, catching Luisa's attention: "We wouldn't be sitting here and I wouldn't have met you, if that painting never made it across the ocean to my country," John said, trying to lighten up the mood. "Cheers."

"Salute!" The Marchesa finally let out a smile, showing her lovely row of teeth.

John was pleased with himself as he was finally able to control an element of his Dream-Escape. After a few more glasses, he was able to relax once more and take in his tall guest who finally seemed content, for the moment at least. They were both silent, studying each other from across the table as two lovers would.

"Giovanni."

"Yes."

"Would you call me by the name, Coré?"

"If you'd like me to."

"Yes. I would." She slid her hand across the white tablecloth towards John. "Touch my hand."

He studied her long fingers as they lie beautifully in front of him. He raised his right hand slowly, concentrating on the anticipated touch, focusing on it, until, alas, they touched and he didn't wake.

"Très bien." She curled her fingers within John's grip. He could hardly contain himself; he was so happy not to wake. He caressed her buttery-soft fingertips.

"Pardon," the waiter said as he filled our glasses with the last of the champagne.

"Merci," he said.

The two sipped the last of their beverage in the late afternoon sun, saying very little, but taking in each other from across the table. John would look away to watch other patrons sitting around them in period clothes, no longer paying attention to the couple, with the exception of an old woman who would nod. Once he returned his gaze to Luisa, he suddenly felt tired.

"Giovanni."

"Yes."

"Are you going away?"

"I think so." He was losing focus of his lover, but he couldn't stop it. He had to let it take him.

"Come back tomorrow, my love."

John Wakes

Sunday, July 19, 1987, 9:32am

The bright morning sun shone through the curtains. I was relaxed and content with my awakening. I eventually sat up and checked the time.

"Oh, wow! I really slept in."

Still in my boxers, I rubbed my hands through my hair and face to wake myself up before heading downstairs to make a coffee and dot down the notes from my beautiful dream.

1:37pm

I thought about her all day. Once every so often, I would get a tingly sensation in the palm of my hand from where hers was rested the night before. It was Sunday afternoon and I wanted to take advantage of the weekend, so back to the gallery I went. It was a two-hour journey from the steps of my apartment to placing myself squarely in front of the portrait. The trip would entail, a drive to the bus station in Whitby, taking the bus from Whitby to Pickering, boarding the train from

Pickering, which took me to Union Station, at which point the streetcar would take me to Dundas Street West where the art gallery was situated. Even though the journey was extensive and the travel time lengthy, I was anxious for another full evening with my new lover.

"Hello," the gallery employee expressed as she strode past me.

"Hi."

I waited for a group of gallery patrons to disperse. I was in her presence once again. When I paced, side-to-side, her body would become clearer and the stormy, mountainous backdrop would become blurred.

"Excuse me," the employee said.

"Huh."

"You're getting a little too close."

"Oh," I replied, stupefied by the fact that I had somehow became within two-feet of the portrait. I stepped back but my focus with the portrait had been broken. I was somewhat disappointed as I felt I had re-engaged with Luisa without entering a Dream-Escape, or perhaps I was and didn't realize it.

"Excuse me," the employee asked.

"Yes."

"I hope you don't mind me asking, but what is it that keeps bringing you here? It's none of my business, but . . ."

"Uh . . ." I thought about how to answer that question, but struggled to come up with a response, as I clearly couldn't tell her the truth. The employee seemed genuinely interested in my reason, as she stood with her arms behind her back. "I'm studying early twentieth century fashion."

"OK." The employee turned to glance at the work of art before turning her attention back to me. "Why don't you buy a print? They sell them at the gift store."

"I suppose."

"Hmmm," she said, turning towards the portrait and then back to me once again. "By the way, I take back what I said yesterday," the employee said bashfully as if she were about to reveal a secret.

"What was that?"

"I said that I think you were in love with the portrait, but I've since changed my mind." The employee's face became warmer as I studied it. "I think you are in love with her."

I stood in the middle of the room, stunned by her accurate conclusion, but I dare not admit it.

"What makes you think that?" I asked. The employee didn't respond, but instead swayed back-and-forth, forming a smirk. At first, I felt compelled to defend my innocence, but something came over me and change my approach regarding the topic. "Aren't you cute." I replied with a chuckle. "What's your name?" I asked.

"Amanda."

"Nice to meet you, Amanda." I reached my hand out.

"Nice to me you."

"It's John."

"Nice to meet you too."

Amanda held her gaze for a moment, but she blushed and broke away. "I'll see you around then," she asked, cocking her head slightly, anticipating a response.

"You know it!"

Amanda sauntered off to assist a new group that had entered the room, blocking my view. I decided it was time to go, but before parting, I decided to gain one more view. I rounded the small crowd to get a good glimpse of Luisa Casati from the side, when her eyes met mine one last time. They were not kind that day. They reminded me of the moment at the café when she was angry with my response. I broke contact with her, took a few steps towards the exit and turned for one last glance.

10:34pm

I sat on my bed and stripped down to my boxers as usual before setting the time on my clock for work. I slid my feet under the sheets, placed my one arm over my chest and the other arm over the other, like I was ready to be placed in a coffin and let myself drift high into the sky.

Dream # 4 (A familiar face)

John drifted through the atmosphere. The journey was always dark and mysterious before he would awaken in his new world, which in this case, was not the Marchesa's flat. It was at the restaurant where the couple last met.

"There you are, darling." She returned her hand in his.

"Hello, Coré."

If was early afternoon. John could tell by where the sun was positioned. He immediately noticed the heat and instantly felt uncomfortable with his two-piece suit on. He scanned the surroundings and did not notice a single man that had removed his jacket. He didn't exactly know the etiquette, but he assumed it would have been inappropriate for him to remove it.

"I need a coffee."

She instantly flagged down a waiter. "Un café pour le monsieur, s'il vous plaît."

"Merci," he replied.

"I've been thinking about something while you were gone," Luisa Casati said while caressing John's hand.

"Yes."

While he sat across from his new love, the expression on her face changed. She broke contact and paused for a moment, studying the movement of her fingers within his palm.

"I want to travel again."

"Oh. Where to?"

"Venezia. You English say it as . . . Venice."

"I see." John became instantly saddened by the fact that he may not be seeing his new love in his Dream-escape, at least while she was travelling. "How long will you be gone?"

The Marchesa, looked up at him. Her expression became intense once again. Her mood had changed. Her mouth pressed firmly as it to stop herself from unleashing a rath of verbal anger.

"Does it matter?"

It was only minutes within his Dream-Escape and he had started to wish he hadn't visited the gallery earlier that day. Then he thought to himself, perhaps he was jumping to conclusions. He was finding it difficult to navigate the mood of this Italian.

"No. I suppose not."

The Marchesa squeezed John's hand tightly, as if to gain his attention.

"I want you to come with me."

Upon hearing this, the heaviness he was feeling had lifted.

"You want me to join you? To Venice? To Italy?"

He couldn't contain his relief and excitement.

"Yes, darling."

"What . . . what would I need to do?"

"Giovanni." She leaned into the table to engage with her guest. "Can you bring five-hundred Francs with you tomorrow? For the train ticket and travel expenses."

John released Luisa's hand, bringing it to his face, rubbing it uncontrollably.

"That's impossible."

He was now overwhelmed by the amount of money it would take to buy these antique coins.

"Coré."

"Yes, darling,"

John was about to explain how difficult it was going to be, but changed his mind when his eyes reconnected with the Marchesa's.

"Let me see what I can do. Give me some time."

"You make me happy."

*　　*　　*

The couple spent another hour, taking in the warm afternoon sun. It was during that time that John was able to absorb her past. She talked about the grandiose parties that she hosted. She would describe the costumes that were specifically made for her. She went on to explain the statesmen and royalty that she interacted with. But it wasn't just that that impressed him. It was her. It was the way she carried herself. She was incredibly confident and would not take failure as an option. She had an incredible positive vibe. Beyond that, John was simply in love. There were moments when the Marchesa would look away briefly, not focusing on any one thing but simply, gazing far off into the distance. That was when he could detect her weaknesses, her insecurities. It was in those micro-moments that he realized how mentally frail the woman was and that perhaps, she wasn't as strong as she led on. As he continued studying her, he also realized that she was older than the age she gave, but that didn't bother him; in fact, that insecurity brought him closer to her.

"Something on your mind?" he asked.

Luisa turned to face him and exhibited a rare shy grin: "Just thinking of my childhood in Milan. It is a time I tend not to think about. It seems so long ago," she paused before her mood changed once more. "I don't care to talk about it." She seemed almost annoyed that John discovered her soft side. "Let's go!" She raised her finger in the air. "Excusez-moi. L'addition, s'il vous plait." Other patrons turned to look at her loud attempt to gain the waiters attention.

She reached into her tiny purse, paid the bill, quickly stood and made her way to the exit. As soon as the Marchesa stood, the entire restaurant turned to view the tall red-headed Italian in her sleek black dress. Her long, graceful movements were beautiful for John to watch. He enjoyed the attention she was getting. He had difficultly deciding whether to watch the patrons staring or watching her cat-walk-like strides. Nonetheless, he was filled with delight as he followed her to the sidewalk.

"Take my hand, darling."

The men and women that passed in the opposite direction could not look away. John would chuckle to himself as their jaws would lower and their mouths would open in awe. The Marchesa suddenly stopped in front of a general grocery store and peaked in her purse.

"Wait out here, darling. I won't be long."

John waited for a moment before wandering along the street, allowing him to absorb the ambiance of the city. He was fascinated by how most pedestrians were dressed fashionably, even though some of the garments were not clean. The smell of the street would change from the sweet smell of a bakery to the putrid smell of rotten garbage and urine.

"Pardon," a man said, passing by and accidently bumping into him and turning back as if he knew him.

"Wait!" He expressed and continued up the sidewalk in search of the man, but was stopped with three women walking side-by-side, blocking his attempt.

"Jeune homme. Soyez patient!" One of the women expressed as John tried to pass.

He lost sight of the man, but he knew who he was. It was the man with the monocle. He searched the street corner but to no avail.

"Giovanni," Luisa called from in front of the store.

John raised his hand at the tall red-head and maneuvered through the busy sidewalk to meet her.

"Don't frighten me like that. You had me very upset."

"Don't worry, I'm not going to run off on you," he said, taking her hand. "What did you get?"

"I have some cheap white wine, cheese and a ripe pear." Luisa continued walking ahead, paying attention to no one in her view, while she towered over the entire crowd on the sidewalk. "We are out of money." The Marchesa did not glance at him but rather kept the rhythm of her walk as she hadn't a care in the world.

*   *   *

Once inside the flat, the Marchesa unwrapped the cheese, sliced-off several pieces before continuing on to the pear. She abruptly stood, made her way to the kitchen to fetch two wine glasses and a bottle opener. She sat, then gracefully, bent forward to remove her shoes.

"Open the wine and pour us a glass, darling." She flopped against the back of the sofa, beads of sweat forming on her brow.

John removed his jacket and placed it behind him, before uncorking the bottle. His shirt was wet with sweat, which was sticking to him as he maneuvered the tip of the bottle from glass to glass. The Marchesa remained slouched against the back of her sofa, staring at him. She was in a different mood, one which John had not experienced before.

"Are you tired?" He asked.

"No." The corner of the Marchesa's mouth raised slightly.

He handed her a glass.

"Cheers!"

She didn't reach for her glass, leaving John's arm wavering in the air.

"Put it down," she said, still staring at him.

He placed her glass on the tiny table beside the cheese and sliced pear. While still leaning forward, he made the decision to place his glass beside hers.

"Take me to the bedroom," she said, raising her limp right hand.

John took her hand, stood and watched as she rose to her feet. He led the Marchesa to her bedroom, which was large, with an enormous bed in the middle of it. The sun was still bright, partially blocked by the window shutters. The bed sheet was tossed aside from when she last woke.

"Sit here." Luisa motioned him to the edge of the bed and began to undo the buttons of his shirt, pulling it off his body, flinging the shirt onto the floor. She rubbed her hands along his chest, leading him to close his eyes. She removed her hands from his chest, causing him to re-open them. She stepped back so that her lover could gain full view of her releasing each shoulder strap of her dress, eventually letting it drop to the floor.

"You were entirely naked under that dress," he said as he studied her long, thin pale body. She positioned herself onto the bed, sliding on her right-side watching John remove his pants and boxers.

"I think you are ready to take me," she said.

John lay beside her, placing his hand on her hip, running it along her soft skin.

"Come closer, darling. I want your body with mine."

He became even more aroused once they were facing each other, with his body pressed to hers. He was pleased by the fact that when he kissed her, he remained in his dream, unlike the last time.

The Marchesa reached her long arm around his shoulder, bringing him closer, creating a longer, deeper kiss. John shifted his body over top of hers, taking both her hands over her head so that he could continue his wet kisses down her body towards her breasts. She released her hand from his, bringing it down to feel him.

"I want you now."

He positioned himself to enter her. The excitement gave him an instant, but pleasurable jolt, causing him to take in a sudden breath. He eventually exhaled, watching the Marchesa close her eyes, her mouth open slightly. The two achieved perfect rhythm, which increased their pleasure. The buildup was so intense for him that when he was about to release; he suddenly woke.

John Wakes

Monday, July 20, 1987, 7:00am

I sat up quickly. I tried to recall the events of the dream, specifically the final part, but the buzzing of my alarm clock didn't allow me to focus.

"Damn, damn, damn." I placed my hands over my face rubbing it in frustration. "Goddamn alarm."

I was still feeling hot and sticky, my erection was still full and I could still sense the Marchesa's touch as if she had just had her arms around my shoulders. Although faint, I could even smell her perfume.

Thursday, July 23, 1987, 5:37pm

I reviewed my updated bank book that the bank teller had just handed to me. I scanned the last row, which read two-thousand, nine hundred and twenty-three dollars.

"I'm going to withdraw two-thousand, nine-hundred please."

The teller made little attempt to conceal her opinion of the matter when her brows raised after my request. I was going to mention something about it being none of her dammed business, but I refrained. She got off her seat, marched over to the manager's office for approval, then returned, opened the drawer and counted the money on the table in front of her, finally sliding the stack under the window.

"Can I have an envelope, please?"

The plan was to leave work early on Friday, head to Toronto, buy whatever vintage currency I could get my hands on and view the painting before I returned home.

It was Thursday, and I couldn't stop thinking about her. The days would drag on when I couldn't enter into my Dream-Escape. I felt that if I continued with these long breaks in between, that I would lose her and that one day, I would try to enter into my Dream-Escape and it wouldn't work. She wouldn't let me in, which is precisely why I asked my boss to leave work early on Friday.

Throughout the week, I made several memoirs of my dreams. I was also able to dot down every detail as best I could of each dream, such as the breeze that came through the open café, the smell of Luisa's perfume on her neck and the noise of the streetcars that screeched while making love to the Marchesa. I continued with such detail as the dust that would rise up every time a motor vehicle or horse-drawn carriage would pass by, leaving bits of dirt that would settle in the rim of my ear. There was also the constant change in odor and the need for it to be written in my note pad so that my memory of the experience would be fresh upon reading it years later. But the most detail, was of the Marchesa, her look, her presence, her confidence while in public and her vulnerability once alone with me. Yes, I was truly in love.

Friday, July 24, 1987, 4:27pm

I made the decision to bring a knapsack with me to carry the coins rather than have them stuffed in my pant pocket, looking ridiculous. I was pleased with my purchases that day. I was able to find and buy seventy francs, twenty-two British Pounds and several silver Italian Lira coins. It took several hours, several transit stops and several dealers, but I made out well. I kept just enough money to get back home, buy a pizza, but little else.

I placed my knapsack on the floor and turned towards the portrait. She was as vibrant as ever. I still got goosebumps every time I first entered the room. I didn't even need to look at her completely, to see her following me, but when I did, I felt an incredible rush.

"Hello, my love," I whispered to myself, but it appeared I was in earshot of the gallery employee.

"Hello?" It was the male employee I had seen before.

"Oh," I responded, embarrassed for my remark that I should have kept to myself. "I love this painting."

"It truly is remarkable." The man stood alongside of me, taking in the same view. "Did you know he painted Prime Minister Bordon and T.E. Lawrence. You know, Lawrence of Arabia?"

"Really," I replied, but was not interested in the painter as much as his subject.

"He was a Welsh painter. Oh yes, he loved the ladies." He paused, then pointed at the Marchesa. "Those two had a brief affair. Rumor has it, that she slept with many of her artists."

I didn't respond. I didn't respond because I was confused by what it meant.

Did she use men? Did men use her? Did she even love the men she slept with? Perhaps she didn't love me.

I glanced down at my knapsack that contained the better part of my savings, almost twenty-eight-hundred dollars' worth in antique coins.

"Anyway, have a good day," the man said and moved on to another group of observers.

I didn't respond. I was annoyed once again by other's perception of someone they knew nothing about, but only through books and articles. I took comfort in the fact that I had met her. Having said that, I still felt bothered and left the gallery abruptly after taking in the Marchesa.

11:04pm

I had un-wrapped every coin and neatly stacked them on my night table. I could only hold so much in the palm of each hand, so that night I was able to hold about forty Francs in each hand. I would transport the remaining the next night. The plan would be to convert the British Pounds to francs or Lira, whichever she thought was most suitable.

I lay in bed, clutching the money as tightly as I could.

Dream # 5 (Someone else is dreaming)

"Good afternoon, my Giovanni," the Marchesa said while sitting on the sofa holding the crystal ball in her hand, before placing it on its holder.

Before John could completely find his bearings, several coins dropped onto the floor.

"You were successful once again. We will have much fun together." Luisa got off of the sofa and knelt to pick up each of the coins. He passed her the others. "I am so happy. I can't wait to travel to my country." She moved herself towards the window, opening one of the shutters, which brought in the hot stale air of the city. "We will travel tomorrow."

"What will we do today Coré? Should I get dressed?"

She turned her head to face John. She looked him up and down while still in his boxers, then turned to face the city view.

"It is too hot out there today. We will stay inside and make love."

*   *   *

While the Marchesa rested, John lay on his side with is arm positioned in such a fashion to support his head while he studied her. It allowed him the time to stare at her without being interrupted. He traced the lines around her mouth with his finger, almost touching her with his fingertips. He brought his nose close to her neck to take in her scent. He wanted to capture every element of her essence as he didn't know how much time he would have with her, which troubled him as he knew his Dream-escapes don't last, although, he had no idea how long this one would.

He positioned himself to get off the bed, being careful not to wake her. He took another glance to ensure she was asleep before stepping gingerly towards the window to look out at the city in the early afternoon sun. It was very hot and humid with no breeze. For John it was like being inside a movie set, a very large and realistic movie set of Paris. The flat was high enough to gain a good view of the street and the tip of the Eiffel Tower.

"Ariel," the Marchesa said.

"What?" he responded, before noticing she was talking in her sleep.

"Perché non hai risporto? Mi manchi amore mio."

John knew the Italian word "amore," but he also knew it wasn't meant for him, so he turned back to take in the beautiful historic Paris and let the Marchesa enjoy her own dream.

John Wakes

Saturday, July 25, 1987, 9:01am

I let my eyelids detach themselves from the glue-like rheum that held them stuck together for the first few seconds of wakening. I had this unsettling feeling inside, as if something bad had happened, but then the memory of last night seeped in. It stung knowing that the Marchesa had a love so strong the she dreamt about him. I was clearly jealous.

She was very quiet after she woke from her nap. It was almost as if she wanted to be left alone and more-or-less just waited for me to drift into my waking day. Whatever dream she had, completely changed her mood. She was still lovely in her own way, giving me a kiss on the forehead before I drifted off.

That last Dream-Escape left me feeling anxious. I was going to skip going into the gallery on Saturday, leaving it until Sunday, but I changed my mind. I had barely enough money for one more visit into the city before I received my next pay.

2:34pm

It was a dreary Saturday and I had become less and less interested in my surroundings. As I peered out of the window of the train, I found the landscape of my train journey so boring that I barely noticed any of it. My day life was so uninteresting that I spent most of my days thinking about being in my Dream-Escape and the other part of my day, just waiting for the day to end so that I could lay my head on my pillow and drift away to be with my lover. I suppose it was an addiction of sorts, but it was something I had no interest in stopping.

The journey to and from the gallery was becoming more and more monotonous and tiring. The final result was worth it, but it was exhausting and to make matters more serious, my bank account was almost nil, but I kept pushing down that little voice in my head warning me of it.

4:03pm

"Fancy meeting you here," Amanda expressed, her hands held behind her back as she approached me.

Amanda's greeting caught me by surprise as I was so pre-occupied with the Marchesa that I completely forgot about our last interaction.

"Hi, there. Do you always get to work in this exhibit with the Marchesa?"

"Funny you should ask. I will be moving to another location in the gallery next month."

"Oh. Interesting," I said. "I guess you won't have to worry about those eyes following you around the room every time you walked around."

"I really don't notice it anymore, but when I first started here, oh my goodness, it would freak me out!"

Amanda let out a laugh, her expression sweetly sparkled as she did. It wasn't until that moment that I realized she was interested in me. I was so drawn to the Marchesa that I didn't even notice how pretty she was. She wore no make-up and was a few inches shorter than me.

"Really? I don't think I could ever get used to them, which isn't a bad thing."

"No. Not when you're in love with her."

"OK, now you're being silly with me."

"I am. But seriously, what brings you to her? I don't believe you are studying early twentieth century fashion."

I thought to myself, how I was to answer this question, so I decided to tell a half-truth.

"Well. If you must know." I started but hesitated.

"Yes."

"I have these . . . these interesting dreams."

"Dreams? Like, what kind of dreams. Are they X-rated?" She laughed, bringing her arms from around her back and crossed them.

"Dreams of being in Europe. You know. After the war. The first-world-war. In nineteen-nineteen."

"I see." Amanda seemed unconvinced. "So. This happens after you study the portrait. That's why you come all the way into the city? To have these dreams?" There was an uncomfortable silence for a moment as Amanda turned her attention to the portrait and then back to me. At first, she seemed skeptical and appeared as though she was going to find a way to avoid the discussion any further. "Is she in the dream? Or Dreams?"

"Yes."

"Are you sure you don't take drugs?" Amanda laughed "I'm kidding. But seriously. I think that's pretty cool. I don't see how that's possible, but . . ."

"I'm not crazy. Don't worry."

"No. I don't think you are. I think it's kind of sweet." Amanda scanned me before continuing. "I still think you are in love with her."

I didn't respond, but instead looked up at the portrait.

"I wish I had more time to chat and hear about your dreams. You're post WW1 dreams." Amanda made a step away from me and them stopped. "We should meet for a coffee some time and tell me all about them."

"Sure."

Amanda waved, turned and greeted some newcomers to the exhibit.

10:27pm

I made the two-hour trek back home. I was exhausted and broke. I will get paid Friday, which will allow me to make another trip the following weekend.

I felt emotionally "off" all day. I was tired and I hadn't had much to eat. I ate far too late and my stomach was upset. The last Dream-escape left me waking with an anxiousness that I was unused to. It bothered me all day.

I held all the British pounds and one hand and the Italian Lira in the other, and drifted away.

Dream # 6 (A Dream within a Dream-Escape)

John slowly took in the fresh morning air of the Marchesa's flat. He peered down towards his hands to see the currency had made it safely across to the other side. He stood and placed the coins on the table before making his way to the open window.

"Coré," he called as he looked out the window at the bright landscape. He squinted as his pupils adjusted. He waited for a moment before turning.

"Coré?" John began to panic and searched the bedroom for his lover, but her clothes were gone and her bed was neatly made.

"Hello." He searched the remaining rooms before stopping in front of the table where he placed his money. On the table, was a note, which read:

Giovanni,

It is time to say goodbye, my love. It is not natural for you to be with a dead person. I know what I am to you. I am a ghost and when you leave, it reminds me of it. I need to live my afterlife without this distraction.

Live your life. Enjoy it with a living person.

Coré

John studied the letter until it slipped out of his hand, hovering in the air like a feather before dropping to the floor. He slunk himself into the chair, devastated by the news. The Marchesa had left him. The francs were gone, and he was all alone in her flat with nothing on but a pair of boxer shorts.

He rubbed his forehead, thinking of what he should do for the next several hours until he drifted back into his waking world.

"Think, man, Think!"

He got up from his seat, opened the closet door where his suit was still hanging. He quickly got dressed, grabbed all the money from the table, shoving it in his pocket.

He started in one direction, then stopped, turned in the other direction, then stopped again, all the while as pedestrians had to maneuver around the confused foreigner.

"Excusez-moi. Anglias," John shouted, hoping someone would respond. "Does anyone speak English?"

"I am English," an older British gentleman said, placing himself in front of him. "Do you need help, young man?"

"Thank you," he replied. He was relieved by the encounter. "Is the train station far from here. What direction is it in?"

"Where is it you will be traveling to?"

"Venice."

The older gentlemen gave him specific directions as to the location of the station and to his delight, wasn't too far. He thanked the man and hurried through the sidewalks and dusty streets until reaching the Gare de Lyon station.

Once in the station, John navigated through the crowds until he found a ticket booth. There was one couple in front of him, speaking in French. The gentleman in front of him pulled out his pocket watch, checked the time, turned to her and eventually placed money on the counter. He sighed, causing the man to turn his head, giving him an unpleasant glance before moving aside.

"Bonjour," John expressed to the man at the ticket counter whom had his back turned. The man at the ticket booth was wearing a striped shirt and vest. "Do you speak English?"

The man turned to face him. "Ah, monsieur. We meet again."

It was the man with the monocle! John recognized him from his last Dream-Escape. Still stunned, he stood motionless, not knowing what to say.

"It is no coincidence that we meet again. I have been following you."

"You have?"

"Indeed, monsieur." The man with the monocle displayed the same crooked grin as he had in the past. His hair was slicked back with pomade and sported the very distinctive monocle. "I've seen you with her."

"Oh?"

"Yes, and although it is no business of mine, I suggest you re-think boarding a train."

"Why is that," John asked.

"There are consequences. That is all I can tell you."

John stood for a moment, taking in this man's cautionary words. "I need to go . . ."

"Yes. I know. To Venice. She is on a train there, already." The man with the monocle lowered his head, pulled open the drawer in front of him, flipped through the stack of tickets and pulled one out. "Monsieur." The man placed the ticket on the counter, sliding it under the ticket window. "Enjoy your trip to Venice. It is very hot there in the summer."

"How much?" he asked, reaching in his pocket.

The man with the monocle raised his right hand, pointing his finger at him. "Keep your money, before you go broke." The man pulled the blind down, closing the ticket window. "I wish you luck," he continued from the other end of the blind.

"But."

"Au revoir monsieur."

John studied the ticket which, on it, was printed 'Simplon-Orient-Express, One-Way, Paris (Lyon) – Venice.'

He wandered over to the platform where his train would depart. He took a seat on one of the benches facing a clock, so that he could watch the time pass. Within the hour, more and more would-be passengers gathered around the track. A couple with a young boy around five arrived and took their seat beside John.

"Excusez-moi," she said, causing john to shift further to the end. "Merci."

As he tried to mind his own business until the train arrived, the boy kept looking over at him, laughing. This continued for several minutes, causing John to laugh to himself.

"What is your name?" the young boy asked with a French accent.

"Oh, you speak English," he replied. "It's John."

"Il s'appelle John, Mama," the young boy said to his mother.

"How did you know I speak English?"

Before the boy could reply, the large clucky steam engine slowly rolled in, causing everyone to stand back as the heat from the engine would exude from the sides of the train.

"C' est ici!" The young boy pointed to the train. A funnel of gray plumage would belch out of the smokestack, filling the air in the station causing John to cough.

Once the train stopped, passengers disembarked before John and the other passengers could board. After a few moments, he boarded the train and took his seat by the aisle and waited for the others to finish boarding. The young boy sat in the section across the aisle, in full view of him. As he waited for the train to leave, he watched the other trains come and go.

The conductor blew the whistle and then the jerk of the train. John was ecstatic being able to finally travel to Europe, even if it was under unusual circumstances.

After the train left the station, he moved to the empty window seat to gain a better view. Once the train left the city limits, it passed through the French countryside. The scenery was just like one would see in historic early twentieth-century black and white pictures. The landscape was dotted with pretty little towns and villas. The train went through a tunnel, turning the entire train car into complete darkness for less than a minute before the early evening sky brightened the train once again. It was shortly after, that he realized that the car was unusually quiet. He sat for a moment, focusing his attention on any other noise within the passenger car, but all he could hear was the click-clack of the car along the tracks. He turned towards the aisle to realize the passengers across the aisle had gone.

"Huh?"

John shifted back to the aisle seat, spotting an elderly man seated where the young boy was. This concerned him, causing him to get out of his seat and make his way towards where the boy and his parents were seated. They were gone!

"Are you looking for someone?" the old man asked.

"Excuse me, but . . . did you come from another car?" John stood in the aisle, scanning the entire passenger car, but to his surprise, it was just him and the old man.

"No," the man responded. "I've been here. You're Canadian, aren't you John?"

"Yes. How . . . how did you know my name was John?"

"Won't you sit?"

"Wait a minute," he said, before turning to walk up and then back down the car. "What's going on?"

"Please," the man gestured for him to sit across from him.

John hesitated, but eventually took the seat across from the old man.

"Where are you going to?" the old man asked.

"Venice."

"Oh, lovely. So am I. My parents took me there when I was five. I was too young to remember, so decided to return. What takes you to Venice? A female?"

John sat silently, wondering what was going on. All the passengers that he witnessed boarding the train had vanished. The old man sitting across from him appeared from nowhere.

"Are you a ghost?" John asked.

"No. No." The old man chuckled. "On the contrary. I am alive, as are you." The old man was clean shaven and had wrinkles that ran lengthwise down the side of his face. He had pink cheeks, white hair and was of a jolly nature. If he was a ghost, he wasn't an intimidating one.

"But, I am . . . I am in a Dream," John replied.

"Don't be so sure." The old man smirked.

John studied him, trying to understand why he was there. His clothing did not match the era. They were too modern.

"Why are you in my Dream?"

"My friend. You are mixing your dreams with reality. I suggest you start living your life as a reality and not living it in a dream." John continued sitting there stunned by what was going on. The old man turned towards the window. "I sense another tunnel coming."

John cocked his head to look out the window to view the mountains as they quickly approached the train.

"I think so."

The train car went pitch black once again. It remained dark for some time as the train entered the side of the mountain. All that John could hear was the train running along the tracks. Once the train left the tunnel, the moonlight lit the passenger car. To his surprise, the young boy was asleep in the seat across from him but the old man had disappeared. The parents of the boy were seated across the aisle beside him, their heads bobbing back and forth with the movement of the train. He quietly got up and returned to his window seat, waiting for the sun to rise.

*   *   *

The train stopped in Lausanne, Switzerland in the early hours and then in Milan at six-thirty in the morning. The young boy was now awake, running up and down the aisles. Every time he passed him; he'd say, 'Hi John.'

The sun was continuing to rise, which caused him to sit up and take in the beautiful Italian landscape. Finally, at noon, the train arrived in Venice. Although anxious to get off the train and find the Marchesa, he waited in his seat until the couple and their young boy had passed.

"Goodbye, John." The young boy waved. The mother gave him a shy smile as she passed.

John instantly felt the humidity once off, the sun beating on him as he walked along the platform to exit the station. Once out, he was directly in front of the canal. He wiped his forehead of sweat and scanned the entire scene.

"How beautiful is this? Venice, in nineteen-nineteen," he said to himself.

"Signore, posso accompagnarla?" A gondolier waved to gain John's attention. The gondolier pointed to his gondola as it bobbed in the water.

"No, thank you."

He turned to search for a tourist or someone who spoke English.

"Excuse me. Do you speak English?"

"Si. Yes. I do," said an elderly lady with an American accent.

"I'm looking for the center of town. Where would that be?"

She gave him directions to the Piazza San Marco, where he eventually located and took a seat alongside the large pillar of the entrance. He waited at the table for a moment before a waiter approached the table.

"Ciao."

"Hello. May I have a beer, please?" He searched in his pocket for the Italian Lira.

* * *

John sipped his beer, thinking of how he was to locate the Marchesa.

"Excuse me. Have you seen a very tall woman with red hair," he asked the waiter as he walked by.

It became clear to him, based on the expression of the waiter's face, that he didn't understand his inquiry.

"Sorry. I do not know," he said shaking his head. "Let me get him. The man inside speaks your language."

"Thank you."

A moment later, the waiter was followed by a man in a black suit.

"Monsieur," the man in the suit asked. "Parlez-vous francais?"

"English."

"Excuse me sir. Yes. I speak English. What is it you want to know?"

I'm looking for a very tall woman. She has red hair and . . ."

"Si. The Marchesa Luisa Casati. She hasn't been here for some time."

"Chi è la donna che cerca," the waiter asked the man in the black suit.

"Luisa Casti, ma lei non c'e piu."

"Sì. Sì. La donna è qui!"

"Pardon me. My colleague tells me she has returned."

"Wonderful." he replied. "Can you tell me where she is?"

The man in the black suit turned to the waiter. "Dove l'hai vista?"

"Il canal grande."

"He had seen her on the grand canal."

"Thank you very much."

John paid for his beer, leaving a handsome tip to the waiter. He strolled up and down the canal in search of his red-headed lover. He searched hour after hour, as the afternoon sun beat down on him, but to no avail. He was becoming increasingly tired. It occurred to him that he hadn't woken from his Dream-Escape yet. He knew that he should have returned to his waking life by now, but was worried about drifting off and losing out on his progress, so he pushed down the thought.

"Monsieur. You need a ride?" a gondolier had asked, showing the empty gondola.

"No thank you," he replied still strolling along the canal with his hands in his pockets. "Actually. I have a question."

The gondolier peered up at John from the boat.

"Have you seen a tall red-headed woman on the canal?"

"The beautiful Marchesa?" The gondolier raised his hand as to confirm his association with her. "Yes, of course. She lives on the canal. I will take you."

He boarded the gondola, sat on its bench and watched as the gondolier push the boat away from the wall.

He was excited to see her again, although he did ponder the thought that her reception may be cool, and perhaps, she would shut the door in his face upon seeing him. It was at that moment, that something else entered his mind; the idea that she may be in Italy with another man. Perhaps the man she had mentioned in her dream.

"You are American?"

"No. Canadian," he replied, shielding his face from the afternoon sun. "How long will it be until we arrive?"

"Maybe, ten minutes."

John tried to push down the negative thoughts of re-uniting with the Marchesa and instead, reminisced about the wonderful times they had together in Paris.

The gondolier slowed the boat and navigated it towards the steps which were in front of a palace which consisted of white plaster with hanging gardens.

"Thank you," he said as he disembarked.

He paid the gondolier and stepped up onto the cobblestone entrance towards the iron gate that was barely closed. He pushed the gate open, causing an incredibly loud creak. The song birds sang and flew over his head as he passed through the courtyard until he reached a large black door. He took in a deep breath before giving the door a knock. He stepped back from the door and waited for a moment. There was only silence, and just as John was to give the door another rap, he heard footsteps approaching. He began to feel a cold sweat come over him, not knowing if the Marchesa will receive him warmly, or not. He could hear, from the other side of the door, a metal latch being released and then another one. The lever of the handle clicked, allowing the door to open, presenting a very tall man dressed as a butler.

"Signore," the man said, presenting a slight bow. "The ball does not begin until nine in the evening." The man was subdued and spoke with a very strong Italian accent.

"I'm here to see the Marchesa." John stood in front of the towering man, waiting for his response.

"Many people will be seeing the Marchesa tonight," the man started to close the door. "Don't forget your costume, Signore."

He froze on the spot as he had no idea what to do. Panic came over him as the black door closed in his face. He turned to face the canal and called for the gondolier.

"Hello." John waved. "Come. Come back please."

*   *   *

The gondolier brought John to a reputable costume store.

"Can you return at nine-o'clock? At this place?" He asked.

"Si. Yes, signore. I will return at nine-o'clock to take you to the party."

It was only three in the afternoon, but he needed to see her, and the only way in her palace was to join the party as a guest. The butler made that clear, so he decided to rent a costume before the shops closed for the day.

"Hello," he said as he entered. "Do you speak English?"

"Yes. A little," the young lady said.

"Oh, thank God," John expressed under his breath. "I need a costume. I'm . . ."

"You and so many others," she said, not letting him finish. "For the Marchesa Luisa Casati. You are lucky to be invited."

She brought him over to a shelf with only three masks.

"There are not many left. You may look."

John shifted through each one. There was a harlequin mask, one with a large beak and the last one was white with a gold ornate design.

"I like this one."

"That one is the Volto." She walked over to the other rack. "You will need a cloak and hat."

He ended up renting the mask with the cloak, the three-cornered-hat and took his seat on a bench overlooking the canal waiting for nine in the evening to arrive.

He began to get worried, though. His concern was two-fold: he was afraid of drifting off and missing out on the Marchesa's ball, but he was also worried that he hadn't drifted off into his waking life. It had almost been two days since he was active during his waking day. This was dangerous territory for him. He knew he was flirting with death. His body would be in a coma-like state and it could be difficult to come out of if he stayed in his Dream-Escape too long. Perhaps this is what the man with the monocle warned him about, but hour-after-hour, he sat on the bench with his costume on his lap. The sun was long gone now and he still hadn't drifted back to his waking world, which delighted and concerned him at the same time.

He could hear splashing from the canal behind him.

"Signore. Are you ready?" The gondolier arrived on time.

"Thank you for returning."

"You need to get dressed. You can . . . there or the boat. It's OK."

John threw the cloak over top of his shoulders and positioned the mask over his face and finally positioned the three-cornered hat on his head before boarding the gondola.

On approaching the Marchesa's dock, there were two large torches placed on either side of the gate with its flames about a foot high.

"It looks like a very interesting party. Good luck, signore."

"Thank you again. You are a true gentleman," he said paying the gondolier the last of his money.

Once John passed the torches, he entered the courtyard before approaching the palace door. There was a low hum that could be heard from outside the palace. It was a rhythmic drumbeat, that sounded like a heart beating; *Boom! Boom!* Silence and then again: *Boom! Boom!* This pattern continued. It was so eerie to him that he turned back to see only the torches fluttering in the gentle breeze. The gondolier had long gone.

John adjusted his mask and straightened his hat before giving a knock at the door. He stood still, listening to the beat of the drums from beyond the door. He let out a nervous sigh before giving the door another rap. He waited once more, but no one answered. He decided to enter the Marchesa's beautiful palace without the butler's assistance. He slowly opened the door to see a long corridor with masked guests lined along either side of it. He stopped, letting the door close behind him. Each guest had a unique mask which were all turned to face him as the "boom, boom" rhythm continued. He was not enjoying this bizarre Dream-Escape.

"Come," said a feminine voice from the other end of the room. John recognized it as his lover. She was positioned at the far end of the corridor, sitting at a table gazing at, what looked like, her crystal ball: her hands hovered on either side of it. She wore a white sheer evening dress, with a python resting around her shoulder, its head stretched out from her arm. On either side of the Marchesa were shirtless drummers banging on a large African skinned drum, which resonated throughout the corridor. Behind her was the butler, who stood motionless behind her.

"Come," the Marchesa repeated, this time, with a more forceful tone.

As John made slow steps towards her, he felt as though he was in a normal dream, where he had no control over his moves. He knew something was very different once he entered the palace. The atmosphere was incredibly surreal.

As he continued down the corridor, the masks of the guests turned and followed him as he walked past them, some of them letting out a gasp.

"Stop!" The Marchesa stood and turned towards the butler, lifting the python from her shoulders, leaving it with the butlers outreached arms. She gradually approached John, but he couldn't speak. It was if he was muted and had to let the dream play out, which left him feeling frustrated as he had no bearing on its outcome.

"Let me remove his mask," she said aloud.

She took off John's hat and Mask, dropping it to the floor, the guests created a low rumble once his face was exposed. The African drums still vibrated throughout the long, dimly lit corridor.

"Be careful, Marchesa," called out one of her guests.

"There is no need to worry my dear friends. The man before me is my lover. Unlike us, he is alive but walks among us. He has haunted me and . . . I must put an end to it," the Marchesa expressed in a slow methodical tone as if she were performing in a play.

"You are in danger, Giovanni," she whispered. "You must wake from this dream or you will never wake," she continued. "It is not your time yet."

John stood still watching his lover move closer and closer, the heartbeat-like-rhythm becoming louder and louder. His vision became obstructed, which further frustrated him as he could only see the Marchesa's eyes and nothing else.

"Goodbye, my love. I will wait for you, on the other side," The Marchesa said, before placing her mouth against John's, finally waking him.

The End

Part 4: The Shadow in the Window

Chapter 1: Apartment 302

Sunday, May, 8, 1988 9:34 pm

I paid the bartender and took the last gulp of my beer, slapping the glass on the counter.

"It was nice chatting with you, sir," I said to the middle-age man with thinning hair.

He rubbed his unshaven face with his hands and waved: "Thanks for the pint. You're a good soul."

"Good night, Jack."

"Catch ya later," the bartender said giving me a pistol-like point.

It was the beginning of May; the streets were still wet from the constant mist. I've strolled along Brock Street many times. Since it was Sunday evening, the streets were bare. All I could hear were the click-clack of my footsteps along the wet sidewalk.

The pub I frequent was only a block away from my apartment building, which was convenient. I had moved into town a month before to a corner building in downtown Whitby. It was an old brick, three-story, built in the late eighteen-hundreds, positioned on the corner of Brock and Elm Street. I liked it because it was only three stories tall with a shop and two floors; the best feature being the eleven-foot ceilings and the tall windows. The building was a brown brick building with a bridal shop at the main level and two rooms on each of the second and third floor. The bridal shop had two large windows on the Brock Street side and three on the Elm Street side and a large green door adjacent to the three windows. The shop windows were decorated with a yellowish style brick creating an arch over the top of each window. The main entrance to the shop was situated at the corner of the building. Above the main entrance were the center windows. My apartment was 202, which was the corner one. Above my apartment was 302, which was unoccupied, at least I had thought it was until I approached to see a shadow in the corner window.

I stopped on the sidewalk, peering up at it. In the middle of the large window a dark silhouette of a person looked out at the street. I normally don't stick my nose into others business, but I found it odd that the new tenant was staring out the window. The shadow in the window appeared to be that of a man, but I wasn't certain of it. As I studied the image, it almost appeared as if it were watching me from above. I broke away from it and continued towards the entrance, stopping one more time to look up. Indeed, it was staring down at me.

John enters a dream

Monday, May, 9, 1988 3:41am

As he slowly drifted into a deep slumber, his body twitched and shifted and eventually calmed.

His dream was not distant though. In fact, his dream was of him, in his room, sitting up in his bed. He sat on the edge of it, staring at the wall until he stretched his neck upwards to face the tall ceiling, staring at its bleakness before getting up. That was when he felt the pull to leave to venture outside of his apartment, to the empty one above.

He grabbed his pants from the wooden chair, sticking his feet into each leg until his lower body slid into it effortlessly. He shifted through his bedroom to his living room, its atmosphere grey and lifeless. He peaked through the slits of his blinds to view an empty street. There was no movement from anyone or anything. It was as if he were the only living soul. He continued to the hallway. He reached the staircase and did not hesitate climbing it to the third floor passing 301, finally reaching his destination, apartment 302.

The door was not closed all the way, leaving a small gap between the door and the frame, emitting a thin stream of light. Without hesitation, he pushed it open, exposing a small hallway that led to the main living room: the exact configuration of his own. It was empty with the exception of one chair in the middle of the room facing the corner. The three large windows were illuminated, but it wasn't from the street light. It was like a warm glow. As he moved closer, he couldn't see outside and the corner window was not fully illuminated as if the luminescence had been partially blocked.

"Finally, a friend," a male voice said from in front of the corner window. The image shifted slightly after it spoke.

"Who are you?" John asked. He was curious, but not frightened.

"I am your new neighbor." The image shifted to the right. "Please sit. I haven't made a friend yet."

John couldn't see a face or any other details of the new tenant, but rather, just a blurry, gray image that would shift slightly to the left and then occasionally to the right.

"I... I didn't notice you had moved in. When did..."

"Don't bother yourself with such trivial matters," the image said, cutting him off. "Please, John. Take a seat."

He stood watching the gray image. He was intrigued by this new tenant, so he stepped forward, taking his chair. "You know my name."

"Indeed, I do: Mister John Randall of apartment 202. I can be a little nosey too, much like the way you were last night when you left the pub. I saw you looking into my window." John was speechless, but the shadow-like image continued. "It is natural for people to want to know what others are doing, when it clearly is none of their business."

He thought about what the shadow was saying and couldn't argue the fact. He was certainly being nosey.

"OK," he replied as he sat motionless in his chair.

"Let's not let that get in the way of a friendship. Friends are meant to help each other, don't you agree?"

John nodded, allowing the blurry-gray image to continue.

"You are probably asking yourself, how one could become friends with such an acquaintance such as me."

He remained silent, but listened intently.

"You are a good listener. I like that about you!" It shifted to the right before continuing. "Back to how we can become friends: Check your jacket pocket when you wake. You'll notice your wallet is missing. You left it at the pub by accident."

John Wakes

6:12 am

I woke sitting up suddenly, placing my hand on my forehead. The room spun a little before my vision corrected itself.

"My... my wallet!"

I frantically raced to the living room, where I left my jacket, shoving my hands in the inside and outside pockets but only retrieved my keys.

"Where the hell's my wallet?"

I returned to the bedroom to fetch my jeans and searched, but to no avail.

"Dammit!"

I sat on the edge of the bed to recall my dream, specifically the image -- that shadow that spoke to me and its fuzzy figure that shifted. It reminded me of years ago, when my mother bought a rotor for the television antenna and how the image of a person on the television would be static-like and fuzzy before the position of the antenna finally set, bringing the picture into focus. The image in the apartment I saw last night reminded me of that fuzzy TV image.

I made my coffee and quickly searched for the box where I had placed the notepad, which contained the memoirs of my past dream-escapes. When I eventually found it, all those past memories came back. I knew at that moment I was still addicted to those strangely fascinating dreams. *Could this be another?* I scribbled a few notes regarding the image I witnessed and his words, excited for the possibility of more.

12:13 pm

"Hi. It's John. I was at the pub last night and I think I may have…"

"It's here. You can stop panicking. It's in the manager's office. Safe in her drawer."

"Oh. Thank you! I'll be by after work to pick it up."

"See you then."

"Phew!" I placed the phone on the receiver of the spare desk in the office.

"Did you find it?" Janet asked, looking up at me from her desk.

"Yes. I left it at the pub last night. I can't believe I did that!"

Janet smiled at me before I turned towards the warehouse door.

I was distracted all day by the shadow's foresight. My supervisor even asked me if I was OK. He said I wasn't as talkative as usual.

The shadow was right! How did it know? What was that all about?

5:12 pm

I parked my car at the rear of my building and made quick-pace towards the pub, anxious to have my wallet in my possession.

"Good afternoon," Jack, the bartender said, reaching for a pint glass. "Oh, right, your wallet. Wait a minute. Let me go upstairs quickly."

"Thank you," I said as I leaned against the bar in my usual spot.

The bartender stopped and turned before heading up. "You want a pint?"

"Ummmmmm... I better check to see if I have any cash in my wallet before I say 'yes.'"

Jack scurried up the stairs. I could hear the creeks of the old wooden floors of the pub as he reached the top. I could trace his movements above the bar as he paced the office above.

Moments later, Jack rushed down the stairs, presenting my wallet.

"Ahhh. Man. You don't know how good it feels to have this baby back in my hands," I said, shaking it as if I were holding a sacred object. I opened the wallet to spy two twenty-dollar bills. "Yeah. I'll take that pint."

6:07 pm

I finished the last of my beer, left Jack a tip and doubled checked to ensure my wallet was in my pocket before leaving.

"See you, Jack."

"Take care."

The streets were busy as rush-hour traffic was still travelling through the town center. The sun was hovering over the west end of town, presenting a warm glow. As I approached my building, I immediately stared up at the center window of 302, but there was still enough daylight to make out anything from behind it.

I entered through the large green door of my building; the entrance was dark, save the slit of light that peaked through the west window at the top of the stairwell. I pushed open my mail box as I hadn't checked the mail since Thursday.

I labored up the stairs one-by-one, still tired from the poor night's sleep, which was further impacted by the pint of beer I just downed. I stopped for a moment once I reached my floor before continuing up to the next one. I stopped once more at the entrance of the second floor, stunned by the image of apartment 302, with its door partially open like it was in my dream.

"What are you doing up here?"

I must have jumped a few inches before turning to see Marty's smug face as my frightful expression must have pleased him.

"Dammit, Marty! You scared the shit out of me!"

"That's because I meant to!" Marty smirked. "What are you doing up here anyway?"

"I... I thought I saw someone up here. I figured there was a new tenant."

"Oh, yeah?" Marty crossed his arms as he continued to lean against the doorway. "Well, nosy parker, you *weren't* seeing things. There *is* someone in there."

"Huh?"

Marty let his arms drop before pointing: "The trades are in there. See? Have a look for yourself. They're re-doing the drywall or something."

I strode towards the door with caution. I must admit, I was surprisingly frightened as I approached it. I looked back at Marty who was still grinning. I turned to face the door, giving it a gentle push to open it. In the middle of the room was a tradesman sitting on a small step-stool smoking a cigarette. He had white paint and the remnants of plaster on his blue shirt and white pants. He turned to me slowly before speaking.

"Can I help you?"

"Oh. Ahh. No. I was just... checking it out."

The man nodded and turned away to finish his cigarette.

"Sorry to disturb," I said before turning back.

"Holy shit!" Marty had his arms crossed again. "You look like you've seen a ghost!"

"I'm fine. I'm just tired is all."

"Maybe you need a drink at that local dive on the corner." Marty maintained his pompous expression.

"I just had one." I suddenly reached for my pocket to check my wallet.

"Jesus! You're fidgety. You better get some sleep."

"I know. I know." I gave Marty a wave and went down the hall and down the staircase to my floor.

"Hi, John," Michelle called from the entrance while standing in front of her mailbox.

"Hi!" I stood still, presenting a rather stunned look. "How are you?" I was able to collect myself.

"Well..." she said as she stuffed a bill back in its envelope, "better if I didn't keep on getting these bills."

She had a thin face, bright blue eyes and long, almost bleach-blonde hair. She had a very pleasant demeanor, which warmed me every time we interacted.

"So, it's not just me!" I said, chuckling.

"How are you settling in?" Michelle started up the steps.

"Great, thanks. The commute to work is even easier and I've become a frequent patron of The Prospect. You know . . . The Prospect of Whitby pub around the corner." I pointed as if the pub was in sight. "Have you ever been?"

"No. I can't say I have."

I strolled alongside her until she reached the door of her place, where she stopped and slid the key in the handle, before turning to peer up at me. "I should check it out sometime."

"Check what out?" I asked.

Michelle burst out laughing: "The pub, silly."

"Oh yeah." I let out a nervous laugh. "OK. Have a good night." I turned and continued down the hallway.

"Good night."

Once in, I unclenched my sweaty palms. I was nervous of the thought of asking her out, even though I hadn't the courage to do so at that moment, but just the thought was enough to make me feel anxious about it.

I flung my jacket on the living room chair and off-loaded by wallet in keys onto my dresser. I changed into a comfortable shirt and plopped myself onto the sofa, closing my eyes, throwing my head back as I did.

I listened to the cars passing along my building from either direction before becoming silent again when the traffic lights turned red, causing me to re-open my eyes and stare out the center window. It was at that moment when I began to review the happenings of my dream the night prior: the fuzzy image that spoke to me and how he predicted my wallet was left at the pub. What a weird dream.

Chapter 2: Michelle

Friday May, 13, 1988 10:04pm

"It doesn't matter," the man said to Jack as he leaned against the bar with the last of his beer in his grasp. It was the same middle-aged man I spoke to briefly last weekend. "You know what, Jackie? I've lived in this town…" He stretched his right arm outwards, hitting my shoulder as he did. "Oh, sorry pal. I didn't see you there." He turned to face me. "Say, weren't you the guy that told me you just moved here?"

"Yes. On the corner of Brock and Elm. You know. That old three-story-brick building on the corner.

"Yeah. Yeah. I've passed by it a million times. It's a great spot. I would sure like to be closer to town."

"You know what?"

"What?" the man replied, studying my face.

"There's an empty apartment above me for rent."

"You're kidding me, right?"

"No. I'm serious. I'll give you my landlord's number."

"Jackie. Pass me a pen, will ya?"

I gave Mike Mr. Sykes number.

The man turned to the bartender. "Jackie, baby. Let me buy this lad a pint, will ya?"

"Thanks. What's your name?"

"It's Mike, but you can call me 'Sir.'" The man burst out laughing at his own joke, showing his yellow teeth and ventilating his nasty tobacco-laden-beer-breath. "Just kidding ya, kiddo. Call me Mike." He stuck out his hand. He was a middled-aged man with thinning brown hair on the top of his head. He was unshaven and had a pasty-red-ish hue complexion of an alcoholic. He wasn't drunk that night, but he was feeling lively.

"I'm John." I gave his hand a firm shake.

"You're a good lad."

"I detect a slight accent. Are you from, England, originally?"

He waved at me as if to dismiss the inquiry as silly. "Ahhh... that was twenty odd years ago. Another life-time my friend, another life-time." He looked away when he repeated the last few words. He peered across the bar at the empty shelves. His body language changed. He became rigid and distant for a moment as he memory drifted, so I decided to change the subject.

"Hey, Jack. Is this the band you said was pretty good?"

"Absolutely. Stay a while and check them out." Jack had salt-and-pepper hair and was in his late thirties. His silver hair made him look older.

"I like you. You're a good soul. I know a good face when I see one." He held his gaze a little longer than comfortable. He tilted his head, indicating he had more to add. "You know. Some people, aren't good. They're selfish. They have evil intent." Mike's eyes widened. "I've met them. They're not good for this earth." His eyes stayed open without blinking for so long that they started to water. He pointed at me before continuing: "Not you. You're someone I could trust."

"Let's cheers to that!" I said lifting the fresh pint Mike bought for me, trying to lighten up the conversation.

"Cheers, lad."

*   *   *

He told me of his job at the metal stamping factory in town. He took delight in expressing in detail how many of his co-workers were cut by the sharp metal edges. He even bragged about the time he cut his thumb so deep he could see his bone under the flesh. He went even further to add that he had it stitched up and was back to work with no gloves on.

Patrons started packing the pub and the band started playing, which made it difficult to continue much of a conversation with anyone.

"I'm going to call it a night, guys. Thanks again for the beer."

"Have another pint, my friend. It's barely ten-thirty."

"Maybe I'll see you tomorrow if you're around."

"All right, lad." Mike patted me on the shoulder. He flashed his crooked-yellow teeth and off I went.

*   *   *

I paid my tab, checked my pocket twice for my wallet and off I went into the cool spring evening air. I took in a few deep breaths and exhaled, watching as my warm breath entered the atmosphere. I rubbed my eyes as the cigarette smoke in the pub was irritating them. I zipped up my jacket and jammed my hands in my pocket, shuddering to myself from the coolness. I made steady strides towards my building.

It was odd that, seconds before I looked up to see that familiar shadow in the window, I had almost forgotten about my dream from the past weekend. I became flat-footed, staring up at it in the center window of apartment 302. I lowered my head and re-gained my stride until I reached the entrance of my building.

The small hallway window emitted enough light to see the steps that led the way. Each one creaked as I placed my boot on it, causing me to pause after each step taken. Once on my floor, I stopped and turned towards the stairwell to the third level. I placed my hand on the handrail and continued up the second flight in the same manner, taking each step slowly, mindful of each sound the wooden steps made. Once on the top floor I stopped, worried that Marty would hear me, so I waited before continuing.

I could see a light beam from under his door. I studied the beam, which would flutter each time there was movement from the other side. I could hear his television set, which I hoped would drown out any movement from me, so I waited for the light beam to remain solid before whisking to the end of the hall.

Once in front, I turned the handle ever-so gently, but it was locked. I scanned down at the bottom of it; there was no light on and no light beam. I dare not knock as that would certainly alert Marty, so back down the hall I went and scurried down the stairs and down the hall. I stopped for a moment before sliding the key in my lock. I was almost certain I heard Marty opening his door and re-closing it.

I clicked the tall lamp on, removed my jacket and boots and placed my keys and wallet on the dresser in my bedroom. Although tired, I decided to open the book that I started; Sir Author Conan-Doyle's, *The Hound of the Baskervilles*, but within moments, my head was either nodding back or falling forward, barely getting through the first few pages. I turned off the lamp, found my bed and slid myself under the covers.

John enters a dream

He lifted himself out of his bed and entered the living room where the three large windows were dimly lit. He paced the room, all while peering out at each window, but his concentration of the strange illumination was interrupted by his name being called from the hall.

"John," the familiar voice called.

He entered the little hallway, leaving his apartment.

"Come. Come and see me, my friend."

He continued down the hallway and up the stairs, past 301 to the end of the hallway towards 302; its door was wide open. The shadow was situated directly as it was the first time they met.

"Welcome back my friend. Come. Sit where I can see and hear you."

He took a seat.

"How did you know my wallet was at the pub?"

The shadow didn't comment right away. Instead, its image shifted slightly.

"Why is that of such importance to you? I thought you would be more interested in forming a better friendship, that is why I have assisted you in finding your lost item."

"That's fair."

"I'm glad you see things that way as well." The image shifted once again. It was as if it needed to adjust itself before forming its next comment. "Let me see your hands."

"What do you mean?"

"Stretch your arms out."

John did as he was requested.

"Open your palms."

He followed the shadows instructions.

"They are no longer sweaty, are they?"

"No, sir."

"Why do you call me sir?"

"I don't know. I guess, I don't know what to refer you as."

"You may call me sir, if that pleases you." The image shifted once more. "Would you like to tell me about your sweaty palms?"

"They're not sweaty. I'm not scared of you."

"I didn't mean at this very moment." He paused. "I think you know what I'm talking about."

"Michelle?" John asked.

"Indeed. The woman that made you so... anxious. Her presence had an effect on you."

"Yes. I suppose she did."

"Why are you not being up front with me?"

"What do you mean?"

"Your palms weren't sweaty because of her necessarily?"

He shook his head and turned his face away.

"No. In fact, it was actually you. You made yourself sweat, due to the fact that you contemplated asking her out. You were so close." The shadow shifted. "Why didn't you?"

"I was afraid. I was afraid she'd say no."

"Really?" This time its head shifted as if it were tilting it to one side. "Then, you missed your cue."

"My cue?"

"Indeed."

John shrugged his shoulders.

"Oh, my friend. Be a little more attentive and you'll pick up on those cues. I promise that she will agree to your request for a date. She's waiting for you to ask her."

He smiled to himself, happily accepting the shadows advice.

"You see; this is what friendship is about. I'm glad I could help."

"Thank you."

"No trouble at all. Now, go back to your bed. You need a good night's rest. Come see me tomorrow. I'm going to take you on a journey."

"Yes, sir. I look forward to it! Good night."

John stood from his chair.

"Close the door behind you please."

He did as he was asked and continued towards the stairwell but was startled by the beam of light coming from Marty's place.

"Monsieur."

The man in the monocle was standing behind the door, which was open only about two inches.

"What… what are you doing in Marty's apartment?"

"Shhhh." The man held his finger to his lips, his eyes shifting back and forth as he did. "Monsieur. These flats are not leased to anyone for long."

"Huh?"

"Never mind, Monsieur Randall. I must warn you. You are in danger."

"How so?"

"Beware of the three vultures." The man with the monocle peered up high above his head and pointed. "They are circling and ready to feast."

John looked up to the ceiling, seeing only the cream-colored paint of it before turning his direction to face a closed door.

The man with the monocle had disappeared.

Chapter 2: The Vultures

Saturday, May 14, 1988, 7:39 am

I made a pot of coffee and jotted down the events of last week's dream: the sweaty palms, Michelle, the man with the monocle and his warning about the three vultures. I had more questions than answers. This was unlike any other dream-escape I'd had. One thing was clear however: whenever I saw the shadow in the window, I was able to connect with my fuzzy friend.

3:25 pm

I decided to visit my mother that afternoon and help her with the garden. She could use the help and I could use a home cooked meal, so off I went with jacket in hand.

I whisked out of the building and almost ran into Michelle, who was holding two grocery bags in her grasp.

"Hi. Let me get that for you."

"Thanks. How's the job going?" Her face was almost hidden behind the two paper bags.

"It's going well. I like my boss and the job… well… it's a job." I followed her up the stairs. "Let me grab your groceries so you can open your door."

"Aww. That's sweet of you." She passed the two bags to me and searched her purse for her keys. "What are you up to tonight?"

"Right now, I'm on my way to my mom's, to help with her garden, then later, I'm heading to the pub."

"Oh, that sounds nice."

I could feel myself become anxious and my palms becoming sweaty.

"Would…" I paused as she entered her apartment. "Would you like to join me?"

"Really?" She placed the bags on her table. "Yes. I'd like that!"

"Great!"

"Ummm... what time are you thinking?"

"Around eight. I mean... eight. I can drop by at eight!"

"OK. It will be nice to get out. I'll be ready for then."

4:37 pm

My mother lived north of town on a rural road. It was the house I grew up in from the age of seventeen to age twenty-two. I had turned over my mother's vegetable garden and removed most of the weeds while she prepared dinner. I was almost done when I took a break and leaned on the shovel before peering up at the bright blue sky to view two large birds hovering.

"They see you," my mother said as she came towards me with a tall glass of water.

"What?"

"The Vultures. They're watching you."

"What do you mean?"

"Oh, I'm just teasing. They usually circle over an animal carcass. They must see something."

8:01 pm

I rapped on the door and waited in the hallway for Michelle to answer, which she promptly did.

"Hi! Come in! I just need to get my jacket and boots on."

She was dressed all in black with the exception of a peach blouse, which she covered with her black leather jacket. I could smell the scent of her perfume.

* * *

The two of us chatted at the bar for a good hour, which I enjoyed because we got to know so much about each other during that time.

She had grown up out west in Alberta and came here to find work. She had no family here and was an only child. She was twenty-nine: one year my senior.

"Looks like the band is about to start," I said.

The bands drummer clicked his sticks together four times and the rest of the band followed with their rendition of Steppenwolf's, "Born to be Wild." As I leaned against the bar, Michelle raised her beer glass in the air and started dancing in the aisle between the bar patrons and seated guests. I was really enjoying it, and even more so, the attention she was getting from the other men in the pub.

"I love the sixties," she yelled as she bounced her hands up into the air, spilling a little bit of her beer. "I haven't been out in so long."

"Let me take that," I said, placing her beer beside me.

I turned to Jack: "I'll take another please."

10:53 pm

We talked for another couple of hours and decided to head home.

I walked Michelle to her place.

"That was fun," I said. "I'm really happy we got a chance to get out tonight. I've…" I looked away from her as I was shy to continue, my hands stuck in my jacket pockets. "I've been wanting to ask you out for a while."

"Aww. That sweet. I'm glad you finally had the courage to," she said stepping towards me. She placed both her gloved hands on my face and kissed my lips. "Let's do this again soon, OK?"

"OK. Good night."

"Good night."

Just as I took my keys out, I heard a door shut on the third floor, which made me wonder if Marty was listening in on our conversation.

I made a point of soaking in the evening with the thought of Michelle and her surprise kiss goodnight. It was at that moment that I realized that I didn't even look up at the window of 302 on the way home to see if my friend the shadow was in the window. I had forgotten about him. I wanted to thank him for his encouragement to ask her on a date.

Thursday, May, 19, 1988 7:03pm

"Hey, Jack. A pint please."

"You got it!"

I glanced at the spot where Mike normally sits. I saw half a beer and a pack of cigarettes on the bar.

"Is Mike here?"

"Yeah. He's probably using the men's room."

I nodded and took a sip of my freshly poured beer and scanned the surroundings of the bar. It was still early and dinner patrons were just strolling in.

"There he is!" I heard Mike say from behind me, placing his hand on my shoulder.

"Hey, Mike!" I took another sip.

"I just got good news. The apartment's mine."

"Congrats."

"You're a good lad you are. Cheers!"

"Cheers."

"Jackie. Pour me another pint, will ya?" How's yours, lad?"

"I'm good."

Mike gulped the last of his beer, grabbed his fresh one, turned his back to Jack and placed his hand on my shoulder.

"Come. Let's talk over here," he said tilting his head towards a small table in the other room beside the bar.

"You know. You're the only person that's been kind to me since I've arrived in this country, twenty odd years ago." He looked side-to-side as if he were going to reveal something of importance. He leaned in: "Come in. Closer."

I did.

"I need to confess something. I trust you and I've never trusted anyone before like I have with you, so I'm going to make a confession. It's been on my mind for a long, long time."

"Yes," I responded. I was frightful as to what the confession could be.

"I once killed a man."

I leaned back in my chair. My first thought was to bolt out of the pub, but I couldn't.

"It was a long time ago. This bloke jumped me with a knife. It was self-defense. It was either him or me." Mike leaned in. "Not a day goes by when I don't think of it. I wish it never happened."

Still stunned by the news, I was lost for what to say next. I had to pretend like I was not in shock and continued with the conversation as normal.

"Is that why you left England?"

"Yes, lad. To start a new life. I'd be in prison if I'd stayed there."

I had difficulty maintaining eye contact with him.

"Phew!" I let out a breath. 'I don't know what to say."

"Just. You know. Keep it to yourself."

"I understand."

My pace was very slow on the walk home. I felt completely defeated. I let a killer into my building putting Michelle and I in danger.

I peered up at the third floor of my building to see the familiar shadow staring down at me.

9:16 pm

I was anxious all night. I changed into my pajamas and picked up my book and started reading where I left off. I was at the part where Watson was on his journey to Baskerville Hall and the carriage was stopped by a mounted soldier looking for an escaped convict by the name of *Selden, the Notting Hill murderer*. I put the book down and searched under my bottom kitchen cabinet for my bottle of whiskey, which I took a quick shot of. I picked up a magazine and tried to find a light-hearted story until I dozed off.

John enters a dream

"Are ya still here?"

John turned his head to meet eyes with a man of about the same age as him. He had brown hair, a pale face and a strong English accent. He wore a faded jean jacket with a ragged green work shirt underneath. His eyes were rather piercing and uncomfortable to peer into.

"What?" John replied, straightening himself.

He was still feeling dozy from his transformation into his dream-escape. He was in a crowded bar, but it wasn't his familiar pub. It was an old English pub which was dimly lit. He scanned the surroundings -- the long bar that curved away from him and towards the entrance, which was two black doors. On either side of the doors was a large window with horizontal muntin bars separating the square-shaped panels of glass.

"Focus, John. It's me."

John looked at the man, unclear as to what he was referring to.

"Who are you?"

"Ya know me in your past dreams as, sir. My real name is Gerald. I'm the one who helped you find your wallet."

"Where the hell are we?"

"We're in London. This is my pub." Gerald was very intense. His actions were jerky and quick as if he were just agitated by something or someone

"You don't sound the same," John replied. "You have an accent."

"Yeah. I guess I did."

"I don't understand."

"What'll it be, boys?" called out a rosy-cheeked man from across the bar. He was a stout man who wore suspenders, had large white sideburns and a comb-over.

"Two pints a' Guinness, Freddy," Gerald replied.

John scanned the pub, checking out all the patrons, their clothing and their hair style.

"What year is this?"

"Nineteen-sixty-seven, mate. It was an important year for me." Gerald looked at my attire. "You don't exactly fit in with your modern fashion. I'm not sure if I like it." He chuckled to himself before our bartender approached the two with their drinks.

"Gerry," the bartender said, sliding our glasses over, then leaning towards my friend. "He was in tonight, lookin' for you. Don't want any trouble here tonight."

"I promise you. Nothin's gonna happen. Cross my heart."

"Good lad. This one looks more like the type you should be makin' pals with," he said pointing to John.

"What is he talking about?"

"Cheers, mate!" Gerald took a sip and wiped his mouth. "I was involved in a gang. We were mates." He unbuttoned the top of his shirt, pulled it open to the right, exposing a tattoo of a vulture. "We were called The Vultures."

John's stunned look caused Gerald to pause.

"Are ya with me, mate? Concentrate."

"Yes, I'm following."

He buttoned his shirt and continued: "We were trouble makers. We did… ya know, break ins, petty crimes, that kind of thing… to gain a few quid here and there. Nothing big." Gerald cleared his throat. "One day, I had a job opportunity, selling some... let's just say, product. Well, I earned a monkey and..."

"A what?"

"A monkey. Five hundred quid."

"Go on."

"Well, these ..." he paused and looked away bitterly -- "so-called mates of mine wanted a cut. They said it was every bit there's as it was mine. They claimed that we were, you know, part of the group. Well, I wasn't havin' any part of that and told them to piss off!"

"And?"

"They were after me. They wanted their cut. Silly bastards. Some friends they were."

Just as John was to inquire further, he felt a gentle touch of a hand on his shoulder.

"Gerry, Gerry, Gerry. Aren't you going to introduce me to your new friend?"

John turned to see a petite woman with long strawberry-blonde hair and big blue eyes, which were decorated with long false eyelashes. She wore a short skirt and a matching bright blue blazer.

"Hello, Darlene. Fancy meetin' you here. This is my new friend, Mr. John Randall," Gerald said straitening himself up as to imitate that of a butler making an announcement.

Darlene stretched out her hand to greet him: "Nice to meet you, John Randall."

"Nice to meet you too."

"Lovely accent," she said. "Where are you from?"

"Canada. From a town called Whitby, just outside of Toronto."

"Oh, like the name of the pub?"

"What do you mean?" John asked.

"This pub. This is The Prospect of Whitby, one of the oldest pubs in London."

John turned to his friend: "The name of this pub is The Prospect of Whitby, too?"

Gerald turned away and took a sip of his beer.

Darlene tilted her head to one side: "You have a pub with the same name. Isn't that a coincidence?"

"Yes. Very," John answered.

"Listen, sweetheart," Gerald interrupted. "Let the two of us finish our meeting, OK, darlin'? We'll come over when were done. We've got business of our own here."

"Fine. I'm just over there, when you're done Mr. Businessman."

Darlene returned to her table with her group of friends.

"Get your mind off that bird for a minute. I need your help."

"All right. I'm listening. How can I help?"

"Ya see, I'm a dead man. I brought you here for a reason."

"What? Why?"

"Because. This is something I couldn't tell you. I wanted you to re-live it with me.

"Live what?"

"The last part of my life."

"Huh?"

"I want my life back. You see. My life was taken . . . or should I say, *will* be taken once I finish this pint and leave this here pub. You've met my killer. Yes mate. Mike's his name. We were part of The Vultures. For the record, his story about him being ambushed is bullshit. He was the once stalking me."

John stood silent, taking in the information. Gerald pointed his finger towards him. "You, my friend can help me."

"How do you suppose I'll be able to do that?"

"This is my chance to change the past. Be my guard, so-to-speak. He won't attack me with you around."

"Wow! I'm not so sure."

"You kind of have no choice." He swallowed the last of his beer. "Once I up and leave, he's going to kill me if you don't come. Besides, I thought you were my friend. Have you forgotten the help I've given you?"

"No. I haven't."

John was worried about the danger involved, but there was potentially a positive outcome that would come out of this. If he could stop Gerald from getting killed, it would also relieve Mike from his guilt that he had carried for so many years.

"OK. I'm coming."

"Freddy!" Gerald slid some coins towards the bartender. "A shot of JD and keep the change!"

Gerald became fidgety and intense while waiting for his whiskey, tapping his finger tips on the top of the bar.

He quickly downed the shot: "Let's go, mate!"

Gerald turned away quickly and marched through the bar as if he were on a mission, recklessly bumping into other patrons.

The street just outside the pub was lined with brick, still wet from the rain. Gerald didn't acknowledge John, instead turned quickly to his left, his arms open like a gunslinger's stance.

He took off so quickly that he was several paces ahead of him, which was when John spied two silhouettes at the end of the street walking towards them, one of them much taller than the other.

"Who's that?"

"That's them. Charlie and Mike."

"Them? Gerald! Just give them their cut," John called and then sped ahead, finally beside him.

"Not a chance."

John was feeling the stress of the situation as his English friend had no intention of backing down. Gerald pulled out a knife from his jacket, quickening his pace.

"You get in the way of Charlie, the tall lanky one. I'll look after Mike."

"No. Just give them the money and walk away."

"So, you bastards are waiting for me, are ya?" he called, charging towards Mike with the knife, but Charlie kicked his arm, knocking the knife out of his grip and causing him to lose his footing, falling backwards onto the wet bricks.

The knife clinked as it bounced on the street. John rushed towards Charlie, pushing him against the wall.

"Stay there."

John turned to see Mike with the knife in his hand, his right knee pressed against Gerald's chest.

"Mike. No. Don't!"

"Who the hell are you?" Mike replied.

"You'll regret it! Don't do it."

John released Charlie and ran towards Mike who immediately stood.

"Back off, ya little puke."

"Gerry!" Darlene called from in front of the pub.

"Stay away," Gerald yelled.

John's neck was quickly locked by Charlie's arm, choking him, followed by a cold sharp object entering his abdomen, the force making it impossible for him to breathe.

John fell to the ground holding the knife wedged in his stomach. Mike and Charlie quickly fled.

Gerald knelt over him as a rush of people gathered around, watching hopelessly as John drifted into his waking world and ultimately to the other side.

The End

Made in the USA
Columbia, SC
23 December 2021

51177104R10146